MICHAEL ROSEN
FARCE MAJEURE
THE BORIS LETTERS VOL II

ILLUSTRATED BY ZOOM ROCKMAN

Seven Arches
Publishing

Published in 2023
By Seven Arches Publishing
The Flat, New Inn Farm Beckley, Oxford, OX3 9TY
www.sevenarchespublishing.co.uk

Copyright © Michael Rosen

Illustrations © Zoom Rockman

The moral right of the author has been asserted.
The moral rights of both illustrators have been asserted.

All rights reserved. No part of this publication may be reproduced, stored in a retrieval system, or transmitted, in any form or by any means, electronic, mechanical, photocopying, recording or otherwise, without the prior permission of the publisher in writing.

A catalogue record for this book is available from
the British Library.

Cover design and typesetting by Alan McGlynn

Printed in Great Britain by 4Edge Ltd, Hockley

ISBN 978-1-7393302-0-0

Michael Rosen has written at least 200 books since 1974 when his first book of poems was published with illustrations by Quentin Blake.

You can find all his books listed on his website:
www.michaelrosen.co.uk

Here are just a few:

Many Different Kinds of Love
A Story of life, death and the NHS

Getting Better: Life lessons on going under, getting over, getting through it
A Guardian book of 2023
A BBC Book of 2023

Please Write Soon
Shortlisted for the Historical Association Young Quills Award

So They Call You Pisher! A Memoir

We're Going on a Bear Hunt

Michael Rosen's Sad Book

Goldilocks and the Three Crocodiles

Ready for Spaghetti – Funny Poems for Funny Kids

Chocolate Cake

Unexpected Twist

I am Wriggly

The Laugh Out Loud Joke Book

This is the second collection of Michael Rosen's tweets that parody messages coming supposedly from the former leader of the Conservative Party and Prime Minster of the UK, Boris Johnson. They chronicle the moment in July 2022 when he was forced to resign by his own cabinet ministers, through the leadership of Liz Truss and then Rishi Sunak, to just 12 months later in July 2023. Boris Johnson is still a member of parliament, albeit a back-bencher, trying at all possible moments to grab the headlines.

However, because the tweets are composed by Michael Rosen, nothing is quite what it seems. Yes 'The Boris Letters Volume II' is a satire; sometimes a sardonic satire on the machinations of the unelected persons in power, but there are also other things going on. Mr. Rosen loves playing games, especially games that involve words, so he tempts others to join in and in this edition, unlike the first, you might find some tweets included by his regular followers who have understood the game.

'For Emma'

MICHAEL ROSEN

•

Aug 1, 2022

Dear Mogg
I have to admit it: moments of melancholy, the sunset on my brilliant career, and I must go forth like Icarus, and find other ways to lead my people to the Promised Hand. In the end – hah – I was caught in an Accordion Knot.
Testes in vice
Boris

FARCE MAJEURE

Early in June 2022 more than 54 Conservative members of parliament submitted no-confidence letters in respect of Boris Johnson's leadership to Graham Brady, the Chair of the 1922 Committee. This committee represents the back-benchers of the party. Many felt the different scandals, including those involving sexual allegations had come about because of Boris Johnson's lax attitude to morals. The number of letters submitted allowed for a vote. On the 6th June such a vote was put to members of parliament. Boris Johnson survived this vote.

However, only a few short weeks elapsed before Boris Johnson, ignoring warnings by advisors, promoted Chris Pincher to Deputy Chief Whip, a position of some importance with power and standing in the parliamentary party. The newspapers were watching Chris Pincher closely but it was a young newly appointed female journalist working for The Sun who broke the news that a Tory MP had resigned his role as deputy chief whip after a boozy evening at the Carlton Club. Chris Pincher said he had drunk too much and embarrassed himself. However, it was alleged that he had grabbed a man in the groin; something he was apparently known to have done before. This scandal was magnified by the fact that Boris Johnson denied that he had been warned about Chris Pincher's previous bad behaviour. This was clearly not the case and first Sajid Javid, the Health Secretary resigned. Saying in the House of Commons: 'Enough is enough'. Meaning that he had given Boris Johnson the benefit of the doubt on many occasions but now he had to accept that he could not trust the Prime Minister's words. Other less influential ministers resigned and then the Chancellor of the Exchequer, Rishi Sunak joined those resigning and consequently, Boris Johnson no longer had a functioning government and tendered his resignation to the Queen.

It was now the job of the Conservative party members to vote for the next leader of their party who would automatically become prime minister. A process of candidates putting themselves forward for nomination would follow with Boris Johnson staying at Number 10 Downing Street acting as

'Caretaker' until the new Prime Minister could be asked by the Queen to form a government.

> **"She has the boldness, vision and strength of conviction to build on what Boris began. That is why today the Mail backs Liz Truss for leader"**
>
> Daily Mail - Aug 3, 2022

Aug 7, 2022

Dear Sunak
Go easy on value-for-money with universities. The hacks will look at Tory front bench degrees and we'll end up with faces on our eggs, like Medusa as she had only one eye. I benefitted from knowing everything about Classics though.
Nivea in intergluteal cleftus
Boris

Aug 18, 2023

Dear Liz
You know and I know that you're not very good but whatever you are, we can't let the snake get the job. Ergo, make up anything that gets the membership to vote for you. You won't have to stick to it later. How do you think I got elected?
Manifesto testiculi
Boris

FARCE MAJEURE

MICHAEL ROSEN

Aug 25, 2022

Dear Liz
We're rather enjoying our sojourn at Chequers (the servants are terrific!) and it occurred to me that once you're in Numero Tenno you might consider some form of extended loan arrangement whereby my family and I take up residence here.
Semi permanentum scam basis
Boris

Aug 26, 2022

Dear Zahawi
You're definitely on the right track with telling people to turn their bloomin' heaters off. Poor people in this country think they are so damn entitled. Just tell'em to bloomin' well wrap up in some warm togs – ski-ing gear's best.
Radiator excelsior
Boris

At a televised leadership hustings in Norwich attended by Liz Truss and Rishi Sunak, now the last two candidates in the running for Leader of the Conservative Party, questions were put to them both by the journalist, Julia Hartley-Brewer. One question she asked was; "Emmanuel Macron, friend or foe?" Liz Truss replied, "The Jury's out." There was laughter and applause from the audience. Rishi Sunak merely said, "Friend". The next day commentators remarked that Liz Truss was the Foreign Secretary for the UK government and so her reply was not a good response at a time when Britain and France were facing a common enemy – the Russian army that was invading Ukraine.

FARCE MAJEURE

Aug 26, 2022

Dear Mogg
I see that the atrocious Truss has put her foot firmly in la bouche attacking France. Mind you I was always tempted to do the same after I read how Caesar had so much trouble with the Gauls. Luckily, he was helped by the Trojans.
Peri peri in sinus
Boris

On the 6th September Liz Truss accepted an invitation from Her Majesty Queen Elizabeth ll to form a government.

On the 8th September at Balmoral Castle, Her Majesty dies. The cause of her death was given as old age. The time of her death was ten minutes past three and it was announced to the nation at half past six that evening.

The Queen's funeral was held on the 19th September 2022 at Westminster Abbey

Sep 15, 2022

Dear Mogg
Where will you be standing? I'm ensuring that I'm not demoted to some piffling slot at the side out of view of the cameras. The world will be wondering where I am, musing on my mien and deportment, just as people scanned the obsequies for Hermes.
In sol honda
Boris

MICHAEL ROSEN

FARCE MAJEURE

> "An outpouring of love
> A king's grief and nation's affection as
> Queen Elizabeth II is laid to rest on day of
> solemnity and splendour"
>
> The Daily Telegraph - Sep 20, 2022

Several papers showed photographs of Kwasi Kwarteng, Liz Truss's new Chancellor apparently laughing during the Queen's funeral.

Sep 21, 2022

Dear Mogg
Have you seen the footage of Kwasi in the Abbey? The hacks could have sandbagged him for that, and we would have all suffered but hey ho, he and we emerge as unscathed from the ordure as Oedipus from the Coliseum.
In dulci jubilo bro
Boris

Sep 21, 2022

Dear Mogg
Am preparing myself for Conference. I am in no doubt that I will cause a massive stir, members pleading with me to come back etc. I think my entrance should be like a great boxer like Bobby Moore returning to the ring. The snakes will die.
Numero uno in Bognor
Boris

MICHAEL ROSEN

"In a landmark speech, Liz Truss will link economic strength at home with standing up to authoritarian regimes abroad
Freedom begins with tax cuts"

Daily Mail - Sep 21, 2022

Sep 22, 2022

Dear Mogg
Did you like my Britain-not-broken, thingy today? I always punch back in the scrum, don't I? Never throw in the flannel. Mind you, we're going to need a machina ex deus to get us out of this one. Ideas on a postage stamp, please.
Cata fuccins trophe
Boris

The Conservative Party Conference was scheduled for Friday, 30th September in Birmingham. People would be expecting it to focus on Liz Truss as the new leader of the party and the new Prime Minister. However, on the 23rd September, Liz Truss and her Chancellor Kwasi Kwarteng had caused an economic upheaval with a budget that gave considerable tax cuts to the wealthy from supposed government borrowing. This had led to a run on the pound and government bonds with drastic consequences, only halted by the action of the Bank of England raising interest levels, meaning that many now had to pay more on their mortgages.

FARCE MAJEURE

Sep 26, 2022

Dear Mogg
My lawyers, Pannick and Pobjoy, are hard at work firing torpedos into the rigging of the kangaroo court trying me for misleading the House — not that I have an axis to grind. We will defeat the Bolsheviks just as Hannibal defeated the Cathaginians.
Toto coxup
Boris

Sep 30, 2022

Dear Mogg
I'm the greatest survivor in the world of politics since Julius Caesar. When I thought Remain was the game, I backed it, when Brexit hacked it, I backed Brexit. Given the polls today, I'm thinking of dropping a memo to Starmer to see if he'll take me on.
Flippo floppo
Boris

Oct 19, 2022

Dear Mogg
This government is turning into that great Picasso painting 'The Wreck of the Hesperus'. Burning and sinking while those on board don't know whether to die or flee. The disastrous Truss should remember the Beatles: 'You can't always get what you want.'
San Franbisto
Boris

MICHAEL ROSEN

Oct 20, 2022

Dear Mogg
I'm weighing up all my options, one of which includes floating round the US collecting whacking great fees for being incredibly clever and amusing, rather like that great Ancient Greek comedian Medusa.
Oracula testicular
Boris

Oct 20, 2022

Dear Nadine
I read your tweet calling for my return. Yes, you're right. The nation is summoning me to rescue it from the clammy grasp of the snakes and backstabbers. You are like Circe rescuing Odysseus's crew from the pigs.
Fusilli con peston
Boris

Oct 21, 2022

Dear Mogg
Blithering heck. If the fragrant Suella can get away with transgressions, why the hell couldn't I? We are a party of forgiveness not a bunch of censorious woke knuckle-rappers. I seethe.
Linctus in sphinctus
Boris

"Truss was a disastrous dalliance who served to remind us what a real leader looks like"

Daily Mail - Oct 21, 2022

FARCE MAJEURE

Oct 22, 2022

Dear Mogg
I can scarce forbear to cheer at the discomfiture being experienced by the snakes and backstabbers. My prediction is that Ms Bravissimo will be a backbencher by the end of the week. Oh the comings and goings of traitors, eh? Schadenfridge indeed.
Tofu yoyo
Boris

Liz Truss tendered her resignation to the King on the 20th October. She had been Prime Minister for 49 days. The leadership contest that ensued meant that candidates had to have the backing of more than 100 MPs. Boris Johnson entered the field but realising that he was not going to have the most votes, pulled out before the final count. On the 24th October, Rishi Sunak was appointed leader of the Conservative Party and therefore Prime Minister. On the 25th October Rishi Sunak met with King Charles and was invited to form a government.

Nov 2, 2022

Dear Mogg
I see that Chair of the '22 has scotched rumours that I wasn't going to amass a terrific number of MPs to support me for a stupendous return to the top. If Pontius Pilate, Berlusconi and Netanyahu can do it, surely I can too?
Aurora Borisalis
Boris

MICHAEL ROSEN

Nov 5, 2022

Dear Mogg
I see the Neil fellow has got a new show on Channel Four. I know I ducked him in earlier days - I didn't want to be ensnared in his devious Pictish sobriquets - but I think now it could provide a pedestal for my ambitions, like Rodin's 'David'.
Ars longa et longa
Boris

Matt Hancock, the former Health Secretary during the pandemic had been invited by ITV to appear in their show 'I'm a Celebrity Get me Out of Here'. He was reported to have been paid a large fee in the region of £320,000. Some of which he stated would be given to a dyslexia charity. He had been forced to resign from his position in Boris Johnson's cabinet because during the pandemic he broke the social distancing rules by having an affair with one of his parliamentary aides and subsequently leaving his wife. He was therefore somewhat unpopular. He said he wanted to go into the jungle to '…show what he was like as a person'.

Nov 5, 2023

Dear Mogg
Am I alarmed that the dishonourable groper is doing 'I'm a Celebrity'? It is outrageous that a) he's doing it when he should be doing the hard work of being an MP and b) they didn't ask me. My route back is through the public enjoying my bluff charm.
Paterniti tedium
Boris

FARCE MAJEURE

Nov 5, 2022

Dear Mogg
I must be descended from Samuel Johnson the great lexicographer and gymnast. I feel in my bones that I've inherited his industriousness and wit which are guiding me on my new book: how Shakespeare influenced the greats - Churchill and me.
Scribus bloccus
Boris

Nov 7, 2022

Dear Mogg
People ask me do I miss being PM? Such questions make me think of that old Burt Lancaster song, 'There's always something there to remind me' especially the version sung by Edith Piaf. Even so, I should look ahead to pastures anewt.
Tia maria callas
Boris

The Climate Change Conference COP26 had been held in Glasgow when Boris Johnson was Prime Minister in 2021. In November 2022 the conference was due to be held in Sharm-El Sheik in Egypt. World Leaders were all expected to attend. However, Rishi Sunak, was saying that he was too busy to attend having just taken over as Prime Minister and needing to set an autumn budget. When Boris Johnson went on Sky News to talk about his intention to go because of his deep commitment to climate issues, Downing Street let it be known that the UK Prime Minister, Rishi Sunak was attending.

Nov 7, 2022

Dear Mogg
I thought I was terrific at Cop22. Anyone would think

that I've been banging on about this climate thingy for the last 30 years instead of writing stuff about Liverpool undesirables and the like. Oh I am the Net Zero Hero. (Could be a hit!)
Abba in latrina
Boris

Nov 16, 2022

Dear Mogg
Has news reached your ears that I tore'em apart and ate'em at the Bromberg summit thingy? As Lady Macduff says, 'Screw your courage to the sticky place' but the timid lackeys who run these things then grovelled before the Orient.
Cannibal hector
Boris

Steve Bannon was a former Tump adviser. He was sentenced to imprisonment for defying a subpoena from the House Committee investigating the attack on the 6th January of the US Capitol. He did not serve this sentence. He stated that he had encouraged Boris Johnson to undermine Theresa May.

Nov 19, 2022

Dear Mogg
What of the Bannon fellow? Is he serving time at her majesty's pleasure? I of course have never had contact with this n'er-do-well, master tactician, prophet and genius tho he be. All attempts by north London wokerati to link us have failed.
In custardi
Boris

FARCE MAJEURE

Nov 19, 2023,

Dear Mogg,
There's something a tad awks about having to declare these hefty goodies I'm getting for talking cock to Yanks. But beware, my lord, of jealousy; it is the green-eyed lobster which doth mock the meat it feeds on.
Othello franc Costello
Boris

Jeremy Hunt had been appointed Chancellor of the Exchequer by Liz Truss after the disaster with Kwasi Kwarteng. Rishi Sunak kept him on as Chancellor and they are both suggesting that, while tax cuts could get the economy growing, they are not going to move in that direction until after the next election. Jeremy Hunt and Rishi Sunak are presenting a steadying approach.

Nov 19, 2022

Dear Mogg
What I like about Hunt is that he's shovelled the doodoo to beyond the next election. What I don't like about Hunt is that he is earning plaudits from the tribunes and I fear feeling for me flowing away from me as the Tiber streamed out of Athens.
Fluvio rectum
Boris

Nov 19, 2022

Dear Mogg
Have you met this Eton Musk? I'll set up a happenstance where we cross paths and like Hamlet and Mercutio, I'll say 'Ill met by moonlight!' This bon mot will elicit from him an invite to speak and — kerching another coin into the family kitty.
Spongeo glorio
Boris

MICHAEL ROSEN

FARCE MAJEURE

Nov 20, 2022

Dear Carrie
Sadly, there will be times when my customary, long-term, fierce commitment to family life may be lessened by the work I have to do on my magnum lupus about the Bard in time for the 500th anniversary of the publication of the First Portfolio.
O lente lentil
Boris

Nov 21, 2022

Dear Mogg
The Times are saying Snake might block my honours list! He has more nerve than Hamlet's father meeting the ghost of Hamlet. Moggo, remind him that he may be unfamiliar with the kind of constitutional convention I've always abided by.
Mamba in durex
Boris

Nov 26, 2022

Dear Mogg
My mind turns to a forthcoming best-selling tome: my memoir of my heroic time in office, when world leaders beat a path to my drawers. My other forthcoming best-selling tome (Shakespeare and Me) is delayed tho' my assistant will take over on this.
Scribo bogus
Boris

MICHAEL ROSEN

Nov 27, 2022

Dear Mogg
Did you see that I've chummed up with Truss on the wind farm issue? I don't give a damn either way (do I ever?), but it gives me a chance for revenge against Rishi Snake. Mind you, I don't want to be accused of carrying on a viennetta against him.
Petti foggi
Boris

Dec 2, 2022

Dear Mogg
As Caesar wrote in De Bello Paul Gallico, 'We have crossed the Rubicon' - the Rubicon being the Roman word for the Rhine. In my case, it's the realisation that the good people of Uxridge may not return me to the House. I must change plans.
Chancer in transit
Boris

Dec 3, 2022

Dear Mogg
Are you keeping up with me as I wiffle on about blockchain currencies, new frontiers, the invention of fire and Marco Polo's discovery of America? The best thing about my talk is the massive tranche they stuffed into the family kitty, ho ho ho.
Crypto anaglypto
Boris

FARCE MAJEURE

Dec 3, 2022

Dear Mogg
Been following the reaction all week to Matt Talkcock's fervid embrace of Gino D'Acampo on the bridge for 'Strictly I'm a Celebrity'. Many yuks! Reminds me there are few people who can, like me, win what Abba sing of: the public's 'Everlasting Love'.
Vom rom com
Boris

Dec 3, 2022

Dear Mogg
Gorgeous Nadine's 'roman à cliff' re last days of the Boris Empire proceeds. I briefed her with the backstabbers' socks, lies and videotapes and they will appear, albeit disguised, just as Caesar appears in the 'Odyssey'.
Noddi drama
Boris

Dec 3, 2022

Dear Mogg
I see the geopolitics of Ukraine as a platform for me. When I go for the leadership after the Snake fails at the next election, I want there to be a reservoir of love floating over the public in admiration of my principled support for Ukraine.
Frantic salami
Boris

Dec 4, 2022

Dear Mogg
Junior-looking squirt Sebastian Payne has done 'The Fall of BJ' in time for Xmas. These hacks capitalise on

my aura, flocking to me like bees to money. Mercutio could have been speaking of me: '...some achieve greatness...'
Sine cosine sun tan lotion
Boris

Dec 6, 2022

Dear Mogg
I don't know if you're watching the soccer but Morocco have just beaten Spain. What I don't understand is why Spain didn't play Ronaldo. I'm reminded of Homer sitting in Rome writing the 'Odyssey' and forgetting to put Prospero in the story.
Rio ferdinando
Boris

Dec 6, 2022

Dear Carrie
Did you do Harry Shackers at school? The thing is, I'm slipping behind with my magnum anus on old Shakesperio, and I was wondering if you could fill in a few gaps in my research, eg. The chapts on Henry, James, Charles, Edward, George...
Etcetera redsettera
Boris

Dec 7, 2022

Dear Mogg
Many years ago, our Party portrayed itself as pro-family, anti-single-mothers and pro-monotony, but bit by bit - thanks largely to my great contribution - we've become much more realistic and hypocritical. This can only be to the good.
Hormona lisa
Boris

FARCE MAJEURE

Dec 7, 2022

Dear Mogg
The big sports news today is nothing to do with what's going on and on and on in Catarrh. Seems like the England rugger equipage are looking for a new coach. Talking it over with the squeeze as to whether I put myself forward for the job.
Inter lopa
Boris

Dec 8, 2022

Dear Mogg
The sands of time fly from the clouds and peck holes in the ways of men. I refer of course to so-called Partygate. As Portia says: 'O, my oblivion is a very Antony, and I am all forgotten.' My sins become mere cake crumbs on the plate of fate.
Ditto in shitto
Boris

Dec 8, 2022

Dear Mogg
I gather that the thesps hoover up vast tranches of dosh appearing in pantos. Why not me? The same question Romeo asks himself as he is about to kill his uncle. Likewise the song by Gladys Knight and the Vandellas, 'It should have been me'.
Hero in palladium
Boris

MICHAEL ROSEN

FARCE MAJEURE

Dec 9, 2022

Dear Mogg
Am disturbed to see that Rosen has his name on the cover of my letters collection 'St Pancreas Defendat Me'. How dare he claim credit for this great compendium of my witty sobriquets! It's like seeing Marlowe's name on Shakespeare's 'Dr Faustus'.
Impostor in Costco
Boris

Dec 9, 2022

Dear Mogg
It's all Harry'n'Megan today! Which sadly pushes me off the front pages. Harry's an Etonian. I regret that he fails to maintain the high standards that old boys like me set. I was much admired by the Queen, his mother and can imagine her disapproval.
Vox plops
Boris

Dec 11, 2022

Dear Mogg
Do they have players that can get the ball over the bar?
Rugbi Superbus
Boris

Dec 12, 2022

Dear Mogg
Whatever became of that great plan to get the oiks to do Latin? O hang on, did that go the way of all fish? Must have ended up in the bin after little Gav got pushed into the mincer, like that grisly scene in 'Fargo' directed by the Blues Brothers.

MICHAEL ROSEN

Sub tarantino
Boris

Dec 13, 2022

Dear Mogg
I'm urging Rishi Snake to tell the European Court of Human Rights to get stuffed. Why should we abide by Johnny Foreigner's rules? We have to deport who we want to, just as Shakespeare had the Prince banish Juliet.
Bigot in republica banana
Boris

Dec 15, 2023

Dear Mogg
Bravo! You're on Question Time tonight with the delectable Fiona. Beware of Hitchens on with you: one moment he's with us and the next he veers off sounding like a woke cultural Marxist. As Lady McBeth says: 'Screw your stock to the courage place!'
Anti tofu
Boris

The leader of the Rail, Maritime and Transport Union (RMT), Mick Lynch has been interviewed on numerous occasions explaining the reasons for the rail strikes that are planned for the Christmas period. Several interviewers have tried to trip him up but none have succeeded.

FARCE MAJEURE

Dec 16, 2022

Dear Mogg
Finally, the press speak out as one against Mick Lynch. Good to see our side closing ranks and using our power and dosh to really get stuck into him. What fun to see us plutocrats berating him for wanting more money for his members!
Hypocrisi ad nauseam
Boris

Dec 16, 2022

Dear Mogg
Hullo Mag has splashed pics of our family, calling them 'adorable'. Good background press noise creates a feelgood feeling for when I run again after the Party collapses at the next Election. All else is in the lap of the dogs.
Atmos mathmos con lava lampa
Boris

Dec 16, 2022

Dear Mr Must
The book is made up of letters I have sent mostly, to my great friend Jacob Ree-Smogg, collected by a rather disreputable lowlife called Michael Raisin.
Genius in tesco
Boris

Dec 19, 2022

Dear Mogg
The rusty cogs of justice deliver up what we wanted - stuffing planes full of people traffickers and sending them to Uganda. Kicking people about always wins

votes for us. As the Bible says, do unto others as you would not have them do unto you.
Moralo vacuum
Boris

Dec 23, 2022

Dear Mogg
As this year miscegenates with the next, I anticipate screeds of anti-Boris boloney about my downfall. Will they describe it as the greatest own goal since Hannibal was crushed by an elephant? To which I say, like Joan Collins, 'Take a look at me now'.
Anus domini
Boris

Dec 24, 2022

Dear Uxbridge Constituents
I am greatly humbled by the stupendous support you've given me this year even though urgent foreign engagements have hindered my ability to carry out much needed constituency work just as Titania occasionally neglected the Montagus.
Parli coc
Boris

Posted by Shaun Wing:

Thanks for your piffle saying you care for your constituents, this was read out during a game of festive bingo. As usual it went down a hoot, one of the residents laughed so hard her false teeth plopped into her Bacardi.
You're the great entertainer.
UX Cons

FARCE MAJEURE

Dec 26, 2022

Dear Mogg
As the old year holds the new year in its legs, so we hap upon the fact that the world hath forgot the case of Boris and the so-called 'misleading Parliament' allegation just as Olivia forgets Polonius in 'The Tempest'.
Memory tori
Boris

Dec 27, 2022

Dear Mogg
The Times has published a poll saying I am more popular than Sunak. Of course I am. I exude joie de ivre, an esprit de corpse and a je ne sais quoits. In the crisis to come, I will emerge like Shakespeare's Iago, the man everyone can trust.
In loco parenthesis
Boris

Dec 27, 2022

Dear Nadine
As you say, before 2023 sinks beneath the carpet, the eagle of hope will rise above the foaming deeps. As Mercutio says, 'Some have greatness thrust upon them'. In the musical about Annie Lennox, 'Annie' that word 'Tomorrow' resonates, eh?
Gin et tonic solfa
Boris

MICHAEL ROSEN

Dec 27, 2022

Dear Mogg
I'll never forget the message of the sonnet by John Milton referring to his time as butler, 'They also serve those who stand and wait on tables'. From the which, I learn, that we must be modest in our ambition for only then will we sow what we reap.
Risotto motto
Boris

Dec 28, 2022

Dear Mogg
Seems Matt Talkcock is not joining me on the celeb circuit, coining millions talking piffle to hedge fund managers. He lacks Classical and literary knowledge whereas I impress with my references to Shakespeare's 'Dr Faustus' and the like.
Parlio per rectum
Boris

Dec 30, 2022

Dear Mogg
One hurdle I need to get under in 2023 is the Commons Privileged Committee investigation into whether I misled Parliament. But hope springs maternal and, to muster my forces, I often sing that Beyonce hit to myself, 'Take a chance on me.'
Pelvic flor in crisis
Boris

FARCE MAJEURE

Dec 30, 2022

Dear Mogg
You haven't commented on my hint in The Spectator that I may do a theatre tour along the lines of Boris Reads Great Poems. I have no doubt I could fill the O3 with my renditions of the poetry of Cecil Rhodes, Tacitus, Herodotus et al.
Arena coc
Boris

Dec 31, 2022

Dear Mogg
As Lady Macbeth intones, 'Tomorrow and tomorrow and tomorrow', so we stand turbo-charged on the shore of the forest. In 2022, the battle was lost for the want of an eel. But not the war, Moggo. Remember Ben Elton: 'I'm still standing'.
Rectal spasm
Boris

Jan 1, 2023

Dear Mogg
Been thinking how New Labour chose 'Things can only get Better' by B.Ream. It very much applies to now, looking forward into 2023. I sense an oven-ready wave of optimism on the table that will in due course light every beacon.
Metaphor dia rhea
Boris

Jan 1, 2023

Dear Donald
You are so right to paint the finger at the woke

conspiracy who've forced you to reveal your accounts – surely a private matter. I suffer from similar ignonionious conspiracies. You and I are being strangled by the establishment.
Zero tax in banco ho ho
Boris

Jan 1, 2023

Dear Mogg
Nasty story in the Telegraph: only 7 of my hospitals being built. Hah! I am Odysseus assailed from all sides by Goths and Visigoths. Worry yet not Moggo, The Mail will splash more heart-warming family pix soon. As Luther said, 'Here I understand.'
Status quo tour
Boris

Jan 3, 2023

Dear Sir Geoff
I am disturbed that you should question my knowledge of Latin. I was reading great Roman texts in my nursery. If I were to meet Sophocles, we could converse in Latin.
Harmano idiotico
Boris

Jan 3, 2023

Dear Mogg
I see that the wokerati are still quibbling over my great novel, 'Seventy-three Virgins', sadly out of print. Their whinge (yawn) is that I stereotyped Jews, Arabs and other minorities. Apart from Guardianistas, who cares?!
Tofu quic fit
Boris

FARCE MAJEURE

Jan 3, 2023

Dear Mogg
I've explained before that it was a great mistake that we gave up the British Empire. If we had the Empire now, we would have control of vast swathes of the earth's raw materials and we could be bringing people here and sending them back, at will.
Castor et bollux
Boris

Jan 3, 2023

Dear Mogg
Have a word with Suella - there's an urgent need for her to go off on one of her rants in which she explains that the NHS crisis and all the strikes have been caused by people in dinghies. It's complete tosh but it's vital we say this stuff.
Croni baloni
Boris

Jan 3, 2023

Dear Mogg
Beginning to think it's unwise these media hacks thinking they can outwit this Mick O'Lynch guy. They're very good at firing at him the latest government briefings but he's got a nasty way of calmly batting everything away with logical explanations.
Cancel mic
Boris

MICHAEL ROSEN

Jan 3, 2023

Dear Mogg
I hate the way people talk about the NHS as if it's their God-given right to have it. Did the Romans have the NHS? Absolutely not. Were they hugely successful at running Rome, and getting slaves to build roads, and win wars? Absolutely yes.
Ergo ego on phace
Boris

Jan 3, 2023

Dear Mogg
Time to get tough with these strikers. The woke say, 'Hands off! 1933!', but before it all got messy, there were some damn good acts passed by the Reichstag: they passed a law that enabled them to lock up all the trade union leaders. No more strikes.
Totali tariano
Boris

Jan 3, 2023

Dear Mogg
When I am finally hauled up before the kangaroo court which will try to hang me for misleading parliament, I will try two tacks: I didn't know I was misleading parliament; I can't remember, I have no bandaid-memoire as the French call it.
Lubricato exit pronto
Boris

FARCE MAJEURE

Jan 3, 2023

Dear Mogg
Hurts me to say it: excellent rubbish being put out by Numero 10: they're saying there is no crisis in the NHS. Perfecto! It's our job to tell people that what they can see with their own eyes is not what they can see with their own eyes.
Optico taurus excrementus
Boris

Jan 4, 2023

Dear Mogg
So Sunak has come up with 5 pledges? I would have come up with 10. The backstabbers have no ambition, no vision. I offered hope and tousled hair. Where's the three-word slogan? Where's the wallpaper? Where's my Shakespeare book?
Turbo Campari
Boris

Jan 4, 2023

Dear Mogg
Sunak on about Maths to be taught to everyone till 18. People with a good education (like us) must treat state education as our toy: think of stuff and tell'em to get on with it, just as Romeo's father's ghost tells Romeo to avenge his death.
Post mortem in oxter
Boris

MICHAEL ROSEN

FARCE MAJEURE

Jan 4, 2023

Dear Mogg
Wonderful to read the press heralding my 'second act'. As Shelley wrote, 'Hark hark the lark, the herald angels sing at heaven's gate.' Moggo, there will be a time in 2023 when the backstabbers in power will trip and I will seize the time.
Carpe diadem
Boris

As Minister for Culture and Sport in Boris Johnson's government, Nadine Dories had put forward a bill to privatise Channel 4.

Jan 5, 2023

Dear Mogg
I can hardly find the words to express my disgust at how the backstabbers have flushed away Nadine's glorious plan to raid Channel 4. I see her as a modern form of the great Roman queen, Boudicca. Like her, Nadine will overcome the plebs.
Manifesto detritus
Boris

Jan 6, 2023

Dear Mogg
Hacks' stories about me today about how I had to be subliminally nudged into wearing a mask. Who do they think did this: Baloo, the Snake from 'The Jungle Book'? Great book - one of Rider Haggard's best.
Extra calpol
Boris

MICHAEL ROSEN

Jan 6, 2023

Dear John
I fear you haven't read 'The Jungle Book' by Rider Haggard. It is wonderful evocation of a pack of dogs led by Bagheera, whose greatest enemy is a lion called Sheer Cliff.
Tog tiga
Boris

Prince Harry's memoir 'Spare' was causing excitement in the book trade as copies were made available in Spain and there were several 'leaks' as to the content. It was not due for sale in the UK until the 10th January.

Jan 6, 2023

Dear Mogg
If 'twas I at the helm, I'd have had Harry put in the Tower. The Royal Family is the corner pin and lynch stone of Britain. When it divides, the whole country falls apart, as we see in 'The Tempest' when Bolingbroke seizes the throne from Claudius.
Hernia in tesco
Boris

Margaret Thatcher's Correspondence clerk and a Conservative MP for West Derbyshire, Matthew Parris has had a long and distinguished career in journalism writing for The Times and The Spectator. He presents a biographical programme on Radio 4 called 'Great Lives'.

FARCE MAJEURE

Jan 6, 2023

Dear Mogg
Do you remember Matthew Pariss? He's forever trying to fire Kalashnikov torpedos at me, so now he's claiming that I'm about to ditch my beloved Uxridge constituents for a safer seat, just as Antonio ditches Olivia in 'The Tempest'.
Deus ex uuoshin machina
Boris

Lord Sewell of Sanderstead was appointed chair of the commission on Race and Ethnic Disparaties by Boris Johnson in 2021

Jan 7, 2023

Dear Mogg
Lord Sewall (who I hired to report on race) says I said, "The race thing's difficult for me." I may or may not have said this, though perhaps I was talking of my last year at Eton and that 100 yards race I ran. Who knows what I know? Not me.
Victor hugo ludo
Boris

Jan 7, 2023

Dear Mogg
I have solved one of the great historical mysteries: Emile Zola's 'J'Accuse' was code for 'Jacques use' (trans: 'Jacques wears out' or 'burns up'.) Who was Jacques, you ask? Jacques de Reinach who lost millions in the great Panama hat scandal.
Coda yoda
Boris

MICHAEL ROSEN

Jan 7, 2023

Dear Mogg
My experience of masterminding the Pandemic has given me what amounts to a medical training. Today I've helped an old friend who is experiencing severe facial nostalgia. I've suggested he rubs Vicks Chest Rub on his chest (best place to rub it).
Aspro pub
Boris

Jan 7, 2023

Dear Mogg
Beth Rigby (Sky News) says Starmer is having an impact against Sunak but couldn't make headway against me because I'm 'flamboyant'. Exactly! I flamboy away, waving my arms, my hair, my shirt, quoting great Romans like Aristotle. Impact!
Epilogue in latrine
Boris

Jan 7, 2023

Dear Mogg
My detractors overlook how the great British public admire my fun-loving cubolic nature, my satiric jests and my easy-going approach to family life. I love that TV vox plop of a northern chap saying he voted for me 'cos I'm a good laugh.
Quod erat desperandum
Boris

FARCE MAJEURE

A well-known publisher paid a large advance to Boris Johnson to write a book on Shakespeare to come out at the time of the 400th anniversary of what is called the 'First Folio' – a handwritten document that was produced in 1623 some years after Shakespeare's death. It is kept in the British Library.

Jan 7, 2023

Dear Mogg
My book on Shakespeare proceeds apace. I have cracked a long hidden secret: 'Macbeth' is a sequel to 'Antony and Cleopatra' because Macbeth, like Octavius is of no woman born, which is why Lady Macbeth died from snake poison.
Venom ex libris
Boris

Jan 7, 2023

Dear Mogg
Exciting find, shhh, keep it under your cat: why did Shakespeare leave only his second-best bed to his wife, Anne Hathaway? Because he was the Bard of Avon. Get it? He left his best bed to...his Avon Lady, who he wrote about in 'To his coy mistress'.
Tempus fuxit
Boris

Jan 7, 2023

Dear Robert
Lefty woke tofu eaters like you don't appreciate the beauties of the Colin Valley in my beloved constituency of Uxridge. You've probably never swum in Ruislip Ludo either, just as Caesar once swum the Hesperus.
Aspidistra in cafeteria
Boris

MICHAEL ROSEN

Jan 7, 2023

Dear Robert
When Mercutio says 'Some achieve greatness', so do we realise that even the ranks of Anchovy can scarce forbear to cheer. Remember, the Colin Valley is as beauteous as the Cloaca Maxima in Athens.
In loco parenthesis
Boris Johnson

Jan 8, 2023

Dear Steve
I am loyal to the great constituents of Oxbridge. I love the Colin Valley as much as the great singer Lindsay Robert, who has written to me here on twatter.
Rolando ratto
Boris

Jan 8, 2023

Dear Mogg
News is out that I am the Guest of Honour at the Carlton Club bash on Tuesday night. Will you be there? I will of course dazzle and amaze, leaving the assembled faithful riven with guilt that they cast me aside, just as Titania rejects Polonius.
Elena rigbi
Boris

Jan 8, 2023

Dear Heather
Did you mean 'you' rather than 'your'? When I was at Eton, I had a jolly good grounding in grammar, spelling and punctuation which is why I never make misteaks.
Calendar pirelli
Boris

FARCE MAJEURE

Jan 8, 2023

Dear Jan
I am what might be described as one of the poverty-stricken gentlefolk. It may look from the outside as if I'm flush, but all surplus goes on upkeep of my houses, wife, and various offspring who I'm putting through Eton.
Aero lingus
Boris

Jan 8, 2023

Dear Mogg
Was it you who said that no one ever claimed that this Brexit thing was going to be easy? And that there would be teething problems we'd have to iron out? I hear that people are having a terrible time trying to get servants in from abroad.
Pontius pilates
Boris

Jan 8, 2023

Dear Mogg
One thing going for Sunak is everyone's getting so hot and bothered about the Harry saga that the govt could push through any old bit of legislation and no one would notice. It's like the drunken porter in 'Hamlet' - we forget Mercutio's been killed.
Alpha Romeo
Boris

The Daily Telegraph and The Huffington Post reported that there were many in the Conservative Party who wanted Boris back in 10 Downing Street.

  'Leading the charge for the Borisites is Lord Cruddas, a

MICHAEL ROSEN

former Tory party treasurer who was ennobled by Johnson and regularly criticises Sunak on Twitter.'

Jan 9, 2023

Dear Mogg
Tremendous article in Teleg: people saying things like: 'Bring Boris back' and 'he was a brilliant prime minister', complaining that removing me was a stitch-up. They see a conspiracy worse than when Henry VIII killed off Guy Fawkes.
Patella in pesto
Boris

Jan 9, 2023

Dear Mogg
If I had been in Sunak's shoes now, I would have made a statesmanlike statement and, building on my role as a family-maker, I would have been able to pull the Royal Family together, bringing to the table calm, wisdom and drink. My Lockdown Special?
Extra bolli
Boris

Jan 9, 2023

Dear Mogg
I have to drop my magnum oprah on Shakespeare and write my memoirs which I will pepper with sobriquets, Latin epigrams and wicked aslides about people I regard as less talented than me. I'll take the title from that ABBA hit, 'Simply the Best'.
Andrex con fungi
Boris

FARCE MAJEURE

Jan 10, 2023

Dear Nadine
Just seen your tete a tete with this Bob Roberts fellow. What a buffoon! By replying he's bumped up your followers count many times over! It's like Moses feeding the 5000.
Doritos in multiplex
Boris

BBC news stated that: Business Secretary Grant Shapps posted a picture of a ministerial visit to Spaceport Cornwall, which he said was the first rocket launch from UK soil.

But social media users spotted that Mr Johnson, who also went on the trip in 2021, had been deleted (photoshopped) from the picture.

Jan 10, 2023

Dear Mogg
The BBC have put up the story of how I've been 'erased' from a photo. Outrageous! In the original I'm standing next to Grant Shnapps and someone has deleted me. Are they trying to remove me as if I'm Juliet when she's banished to Mantua?
Text fext
Boris

Jan 10, 2023

Dear Adam
Since Brexit, we have been able to relearn that female beauty doesn't reside overseas. We have a multitude of English roses right here. After all, was it not the Tudors who combined the roses of Norfolk and Shropshire?

MICHAEL ROSEN

Rosa bote
Boris

Jan 10, 2023

Dear Adam
Finally. Someone who realises where genius resides. As Shakespeare puts it in the 'Merchant of Venus', "Tell me where is fancy bread, Or in the heart or in the head?"
Piccadilli circe
Boris

Jan 11, 2023

Dear Adam
Nadine is a perfect woman. Think of 'The Birth of Venus' by Michelangelo. Think of Shakespeare's sonnet 'Shall I compare thee to a winter's day?'
Ajax trans enamel surfaci
Boris

Jan 11, 2023

Dear Mogg
The government have got to make it clear that what we're doing now is levelling down. We have to squash Mick O'Lynch trying to level up, just as Spartacus squashed the slaves. Who thought levelling up was ever a good idea anyway?
Orient espresso
Boris

FARCE MAJEURE

                                                          Jan 12, 2023

Dear Mogg
Lo! See how the Left are quaking in their tofu that I will be recalled to steer the ship in time for the General Election just as Macbeth rode to power against Dunsinane. When that happens, Starmer will be laughing on the other side of his farce.
Tarka de otta
Boris

                                                          Jan 12, 2023

Dear Mogg
Sneaks have been talking to ITV about our parties. I brought fun to Numero 10 just as Malvolio is a harbinger of joy in 'Hamlet'. Who saved Troy from the Greeks? The Wooden Horse. I am the Wooden Horse, Moggo.
Crucificato in asda
Boris

                                                          Jan 12, 2023

Dear Mogg
Great news: culture sec Michelle O'Donellan says that the Elgin Marbles are staying. Good stuff: no point in taking them back and hoisting them on to the Apocalypse in Athens. It's mine! as Callum says in 'The Hobbit'.
Pedimenti impedimenti
Boris

                                                          Jan 12, 2023

Dear Mogg
The Times is saying that they've been told that some of our aides were having it off in the bushes during one of

the lockdown parties. Or in a cupboard. Or in the
grandfather clock. It's all in Ovid's 'Arse Amatoria'.
Salsa in chassis
Boris

Jan 13, 2023

Dear Mogg
One scheme I'm scheming: promise Sunak I won't
challenge him, so long as he gives me a safe seat in
some god-forlorn place with a humungous Tory maj. A
quid pro quo like Iago promising to marry Desdemona if
Othello burns the handkerchief.
Gorgonzola victoria
Boris

Jan 13, 2023

Dear Mogg
I'm due for another heroic visit to Ukraine. It'll foster
huge goodwill for me amongst wavering supporters in
Britain, so I will stand in fatigues next to a cannon,
shaking hands with Zerinsky, just as Churchill appeared
with the Archduke Ferdinand.
Ex catheter
Boris

Jan 14, 2023

Dear Mogg
Surely 'tis hugely to my advantage that this Privileged
Committee hasn't brought me to trial yet. Memories
fade, just as Prospero says in 'Twelfth Night', all is
'melted into thin hair'.
In excelsis weston super mare
Boris

FARCE MAJEURE

Jan 14, 2023

Dear Jan
It's a great shame that the great Ruislip Lido is polluted in my constituency of Oxbridge. Why doesn't everyone in Oxbridge go and swim in the Lido in Venice instead?
Mona lisa minelli
Boris

Jan 15, 2023

Dear Mogg
I can see that the hacks are weevilling away claiming that I had this or that stash of cash when I was PM. The fact is that it's damn hard to live off what the state gives you to do that job. Did King Lear survive on Hampstead Heath?
Dua lupa al dente
Boris

Jan 15, 2023

Dear Buzz
I'm afraid you addressed your tweet to the wrong person. Michael Rosen is just a conduit (and not a very good one) of my great letters. I don't make mistakes.
Felix catto pratto
Boris

Jan 16, 2023

Dear Mogg
News is out on me writing my stunning memoir about my time as PM. It's an overture to being PM again, much as Verdi wrote an overture for his 'Marriage of Figaro'. I will fill it with un-PC jests, career-toppling blows and risqué asides.

Khazi fan tutti
Boris

Jan 16, 2023

Dear Mogg
The reason why I'm writing a memoir is because I've learned over the years that the nation hangs on my every word. They admire how I speak 'con brie' as the musicians put it. They know that I am sincere and have my best interests at heart.
Ego in lego
Boris

Jan 17, 2023

Dear Mogg
Grant Schnapps is a jester, isn't he? He's now saying that he told staff I needed 'hair-brushing, not airbrushing' from the tweet. Well, Grant, if you're in high office, the point is to make no unforced errers.
Velux staccato
Boris

Jan 17, 2023

Dear Lynne
I'm afraid you've written this to the wrong person. I write the letters. Michael Rosen is the conduit for them, just as Zeus carried messages from Hermes.
Post op ergo saracen prop hoc
Boris

FARCE MAJEURE

Jan 17, 2023

Dear Mogg
My publishers are being widely quoted as saying that my memoir will be 'like no other'. They are of course quoting from 'Something' by Abba - 'Something in the way she moves, Attracts me like no other lover'. How appropriate.
Toto scrotum
Boris

"Stratford constituents say they deserve better than Nadhim Zahawi after he was reselected as their Conservative candidate"

Redditch Standard - Jan 17, 2023

Jan 17, 2023

Dear Mogg
Old Nadim Zahari is a card isn't he? He has us all fooled, eh? I thought he was as clean as a thistle, seems like he's done some damned fine lucre juggling to keep old Mr HMRC at bay, just as Prospero has to fight off Laertes.
Lax tax
Boris

David Davis served as secretary of state for exiting the European Union under Theresa May.

Jan 18, 2023

Dear Mogg
The mother of all snakes, David Davis, has written an

article saying if I lead the Tories into the next election it'll end up with us being out of power for a decade. 12 years?! What does he know? He's the Cinderella, fated never to win the frog.
Mucosa nervosa
Boris

Jan 19, 2023

Dear Mogg
Vicious attack from the Teleg saying we've flunked Brexit - "almost nothing has been achieved". Hah! Next thing, they'll be on to me for one of my witticisms, wisecracks or pungent aperçus, deriving them, as I do from Harpo Marx.
Quip quo squid
Boris

"Boris Johnson makes a surprise trip to Ukraine Former PM says it is a privilege to show solidarity after being invited by Volodymyr Zelensky"

The Guardian - Jan 22, 2023

Mr Johnson's spokesperson said he 'fully supports the UK's foreign policy on Ukraine.' Downing Street said Rishi Sunak was 'supportive of Mr Johnson's visit.'

The article explained that some people thought it was to distract attention from the difficulties arising from Boris Johnson's finances and the appointment of Robert Sharp at the BBC.

FARCE MAJEURE

Jan 22, 2023

Dear Mogg
It goes without saying (which is why I'm saying it) that there is no relationship between Robert Sharp arranging a loan for me and his subsequent appointment as ITV chairman. The issue here though is how I can lead the Ukrainians to victory.
Victoria plummus
Boris

Reply from Shaun Wing:

Dear Boris
Yes, I found Sharp amiable - especially in reference to impartiality - he's a chomp in that department. The dear fellow was Sunak's bigChief @ Goldman&Sacks. "Parva mundi." As Madonna once said... "Some like it hot."
Smugg

The Independent newspaper reported that Nadhim Zahawi was threatening to sue them if they published the information they had about him being investigated over his tax affairs.

Jan 23, 2023

Dear Mogg
I see that Sajid Zahawi is clinging on. You wait till they find out what's going on just as Magwitch finds out that his benefactor was really Pip. But as for me, there's no smoking bomb linking me to Robert Sharp the chair of ITV.
Cui bonio
Boris

MICHAEL ROSEN

Jan 24, 2023

Dear Mogg
I'm going full-on bellicose now. There's never been a time when flag-waving and sabre-rattling didn't drum up support, especially amongst people who are not going to be killed. And I come up covered in posies. Ah, I remember 'Adlestrot', by Wordsworth.
Jingo bingo
Boris

Jan 24, 2023

Dear Mogg
My visit to Ukraine is being acclaimed because people admire my military acumem. As I tell Zerensky, 'Remember the Rolling Stones, 'The long and winding road'.' I dread to think of what might have happened if Jeremy Paxman had won in 2019.
Stu in pyrex
Boris

Jan 24, 2023

Dear Mogg
The BBC website asks: 'Why would Boris Johnson need an £800,000 loan?' and says that it was 'to sustain my lifestyle', as if there's something wrong with that!!! Did Harry Hotspur cut back on his lifestyle when he became king?
Cor! Decor!
Boris

FARCE MAJEURE

Jan 24, 2023

Dear Gregor
You've mistakenly addressed this tweet to Michael Rosen. I write the letters. Rosen is just the pigeon carrying my messages.
Post officio
Boris

Jan 25, 2023

Dear Mogg
The Telegraph is on to it: they reckon that the backstabbers are trying to remove my erstwhile comrades so that when I make my heroic comeback, none of them is there to carry their leader back to Siege Garrulous in triumph.
Excalibur in rolex
Boris

Jan 25, 2023

Dear Mogg
I'm not worried about what this Commons Privileged Committee are going to dig up about me nor whether I misled Parliament. It's not as if they behead you and parade your head on Tower Bridge as they did in Shakespeare's day.
Decapitato potato
Boris

MICHAEL ROSEN

Jan 25, 2023

Dear Mogg
Do you think Sajid Zahawi will be dragged from his horse, put in chains and brought to Numero 10? He's toast. Of course, when it came to the matter of resigning, I behaved as honourably as Claudius in 'Macbeth'. Listen and learn, Zahari.
Standardi in pubic
Boris

Jan 25, 2023

Dear Mogg
Sunak answered Qs about Namid Zahawi by invoking Corbyn. Seems like he's going into the next election, fighting the last. Do you ever get the impression he's not the brightest star in the solar system?
Arsa major
Boris

Jan 25, 2023

Dear Mogg
How funny can it be that Sunak (backstabber, conspirator-in-chief) is claiming he's being ethical in his handling of the Nahim Zamawi case! As if Rishi is the star in: the only way is ethics.
Plato in nato
Boris

FARCE MAJEURE

Jan 26, 2023

Dear Mogg
Do you remember we despised snitches at Eton? Didn't we get them in a head lock in the chapel vestry? This Commons Privileged Committee (Kangaroo Court) is positively encouraging snitching from the partygoers. Despicable.
Semper salami
Boris

"Boris Johnson's legal fees could cost taxpayer more than £222,000, says top civil servant"

Sky News - Jan 26, 2023

The former PM is entitled to money from the public purse as he faces an investigation over whether he misled parliament about partygate, and he has already spent over £200,000 on advice.

Jan 26, 2023

Dear Mogg
O the woke tofurati are bleating about the bill they've got to foot for my appearance at the Commons Privileged Committee (Kangaroo Court). Oh boo bloody hoo. Do they think when Zeus ruled Rome, it came cheap?
Strepsil tapenade
Boris

Jan 27, 2023

Dear Nadine
Fantastic news that you're hosting this new show on TalkTV and even more fantastic news that I am to be your first guest. Wise move! The Great British People will

MICHAEL ROSEN

see in a blink of an ear what they are missing.
Mascara sub toga
Boris

Jan 28, 2023

Dear Mogg
The Telegraph has a superb report where one of the great England rugger team - Mario Itoje - says that sacking the coach, Freddie Jones, was like my demise. As the counsellors say to Nebuchadnezzar in 'Othello', 'True, o king.'
Ava gardna in pandora
Boris

A tweet to Boris:

Why do all the versions of 'Othello' that are performed these days cut the part of Nebuchadnezzar? It's a disgraceful example of political wokeness gone even more mad. I find it sad that the schoolchildren of today are taught nothing of this greatest of English kings.

"How many times did Boris Johnson meet Richard Sharp? The former PM met the BBC chair even more times than he did Rupert Murdoch from 2021-22"

New Statesman - Jan 24, 2022

FARCE MAJEURE

Jan 28, 2023

Dear Mogg
The Times think they have a scoop: that I was warned to not seek advice from Robert Sharp, head of ITV. Hah! All sorts advise me and I forget it all. Do they think they can pluck from the memory a rooted swallow, as Macbeth says to Polonius?
Amnesia in urinal
Boris

Many people thought Rishi Sunak was dilatory in dealing with Nadhim Zahawi. However, when HMRC state that the 'mistakes' in Zahawi's tax assessment were not an 'innocent' error as he had been suggesting, Rishi Sunak took action sacking him from his position as Conservative Party Chair.

Jan 29, 2023

Dear Mogg
Labour are 200% ahead in the polls. It's a matter of days before our Party will turn to me to pull it out of the drumlins. Just as Claudius wagers whether Hamlet will beat Mercutio in the wrestling, I bet you we'll lose unless I'm leader.
Cogito ergo plum
Boris

Jan 30, 2023

Dear Mogg
Have you heard the rumours? Guess who's being tipped to follow Sajid Zawawi as Party Chairman? O yes, the great Boris himself. I edge nearer and nearer to the throne just as Atlas inched between Scylla and

MICHAEL ROSEN

Chlamydia to become King of Persia.
Manic samosa
Boris

Jan 30, 2023

Dear Sunak
I hesitate writing to you in the light of your treacherous treatment of the greatest man to stand at the Despatches Box but your failure to deal with the Sajid Zawahi matter gave me cause to guffaw. Schadenfreude - as the Egyptians say.
Durablo gorgonzola
Boris

Jan 30, 2023

Dear Mogg
The execrable Guardian is nosing around Oxfordshire in the hope of winkling out of the Hanley constituency some news that I might return. I love the Thames at Hanley always remembering the song that Winnie the Pooh sings, 'Up tails all'.
Post balti rectal chaos
Boris

Jan 30, 2023

Dear Mogg
Fantastic! I top the charts for the MP who's earned the most dosh: 2.3 bloomin' mill! I am the Colossus of Roads, the piece that surpasses all understanding. One mystery, Moggo: where's it all gone?! Down the Pan, god of the underworld.
Sophocles in gelato
Boris

FARCE MAJEURE

Jan 30, 2023

Dear Mogg
Sajid Zawahi gone. I predicted it, like Cassandra, the Roman princess feted to tell the truth but never to be believed. He was like me: decent, honest and insightful. I expect to be recalled. I hover over the empty seat like Bonquo's ghost.
Aveeno con brio
Boris

Jan 30, 2023

Dear Peter
Rosen didn't write the letter. I did.
Facto cacko
Boris

Tweet posted by Janet:

Dear Boris
I think you'll find Sajid Javid & Nadhim Zahawi are two different people although I'm sure your followers will understand that telling ethnic minorities apart is difficult! Talk about racism! If you're going to make a point then at least get the name right.

Jan 30, 2023

Dear Janet
You've addressed this letter to Michael Rosen. Big mistake. I wrote the letter. Michael Rosen is nothing more than my carrier pigeon.
Veritas upmias
Boris

MICHAEL ROSEN

Jan 30, 2023

Dear Mogg
One of our soft soap merchants was blathering away on World at Once. Why do we send these witterers out there to say that Sunak's done the 'right thing' and it's time to move on. I have trouble holding down a mix of vodka and brandy but that! Eurch!
Broccoli detox
Boris

Jan 30, 2023

Dear Mogg
Everyone wants to know about my tete-de-tete with Putin. The world's hacks are beating a path to my drawer to hear about what I say that Putin said (do I really remember? Nope.), while the Party piffle about with Sajid Zadawi's misspeaks.
Swarfega in scrotum
Boris

Posted by Ken MacIver@mac499:

Technical note:- Swarfega used to make an orange coloured and scented hand cleaner with granular 'bits' in to help cut through the muck.. Ps do not confuse with ralgex in scrotum a totally different experience...

FARCE MAJEURE

Jan 30, 2023

Dear Mogg
Did you hear the Today programme? The Party wheeled out some hapless wench - the wokerati will say that's sexist - bah! - and she was eviscerated by the interviewer. When I was on, Robinson told me to stop talking. What chutzpah! as the French say.
Inebrio aurora
Boris

Jan 31, 2023

Dear Mogg
You were superb talking to Katy Burley when you said that 'we shouldn't be too snowlflakey' about bullying. Exactly, we're being bulldozed by woke snowflakerati whingeing about a bit of red meat passion. Bullying - pah!
Uber pussi
Boris

Jan 31, 2023

Dear Matt Talkcock
I watched you on @GMB this morning really doing a good job for us, blathering away about nothing, coming over as a psychopath but nice with it, which is exactly the combo we need at the moment.
Lucre euphoria
Boris

MICHAEL ROSEN

Feb 1, 2023

Dear Mogg
Worst performing economy! The wokerati will try to blame me but it can hardly be my fault as I know zero minus zero about economics beyond what Thelonius says to Hamlet: 'Neither a borrower nor a lender be.'
Polyfilla con pomodoro
Boris

Feb 1, 2023

Dear Mogg
The great Roman poet Juventus asked 'Quis custodiet ipsos custardies?' a pertinent question to ask of this government! I predict the party will recall me, for the words of the profit are written on the subway walls as Sonny and Cher told us.
Revertigo impetigo
Boris

Reply from Longhouses:

I guess that you are referring to Decimus Junius Juvenalis, usually referred to in Anglo-English as Juvenal? The tag you are looking for is, "Quis custodiet ipsos custodes".

FARCE MAJEURE

Feb 1, 2023

Dear Longhouses
You've written to Michael Rosen who is merely my carrion pigeon. I write the letters. My Latin is without blemish. As am I.
Episstolari marvello
Boris

Feb 1, 2023

Dear Mogg
I think Sunak's in trouble. The point is Numero 10 have denied that he was told formally about Raab's bully boy stuff. This leaves the drawer open for him having had it whispered to him. Praps Raab is Sylvester Stallone as when he played 'Raging Bull'.
Blotto voce
Boris

Feb 1, 2023

Dear Mogg
I sing to myself the old song, 'Some talk of Alexander, and some of Sophocles of Lector and my sander, and such great names as these' because 1 day, there'll be songs about my greatness because, as First folio reminds us, 'Some are born great.'
Laxativo excessivo
Boris

MICHAEL ROSEN

Feb 1, 2023

Dear Nadine
The Guardian has leaked your splendid interview with me, soon to be aired on TVTalk channel. Thanks to you and your beautifully gracious ways, we will reveal that talk of a breech of rules is piffle. The upcoming Kangaroo Court will implode.
Exoneratio on patio
Boris

Feb 1, 2023

Dear Mogg
As I survey the many possibs of future career moves, it occurs to me I could do an Eisenhower. He went from being President to being a general, so why not me? After all, I studied the Penelopennesian War (named after Penelope in the Odyssey).
Hic hoc ac ac
Boris

Feb 1, 2023

Dear Mogg
Are you tracking me on my Ukraine pronouncements? I'm going all out for fighter jets now and that shows yet again how weak Sunak is. Fighter jets are great. Eeeeeoowwww! Bang bang bang! Mad Max von Richthofen. Zap zap zap!
Conflagratio super super
Boris

FARCE MAJEURE

Feb 1, 2023

Dear Mogg
Frightful time: millions of workers on strike. If Sunak wasn't such a weed, he'd arrest union leaders like Mick O'Lynch and ban strikes. My jovial good-chap style would win over doubters. I'm a winner. Abba said it right: 'Simply the best'.
Modest algae
Boris

Boris Johnson had a speaking engagement in the United States.

Feb 1, 2023

Dear Mogg
Outrageous intrusion into my private finances: officials examining the decision to provide £220k of taxpayers' money to fund my legal defence at the Partygate Kangaroo Court! I say ta! Am minded of 'Thank you for the music' by Bucks Fizz.
Surplus moola con
Boris

SteveHill200 replying to @MichaelRosenYes:

I am impressed that even when out of the country again Boris takes the time to reply to comments

Feb 2, 2023

Dear Mogg
I'm doing a lot of ear-bashing in the US, telling them to pull their fingers out and send in the jets. Gotta give it to Blair, he grasped the metal, told'em what to do and they

did it. Stevie Smith put it his way, 'Not wavering but drowning.'
Aviva espana
Boris

Feb 2, 2023

Dear Mogg
Tiresome hacks are still weevilling about trying to find foul play over that loan I copped. How would I remember? I was probs on to my fifth Courvoisier by then. We are such stuff as dreams are made on, as Aspro says in 'The Tempest'.
Stupor in brasso
Boris

Feb 2, 2023

Dear Mogg
I'm often minded of the character of Firstfolio in 'Twelfth Night', when he turns on the revellers and says, 'My Masters are you mad?' Instead of bringing me in from the gold, they leave me outside faraging about looking for scraps.
Sole miami
Boris

Unknown Tweeter/follower:

Faraging? A new word for scraping the barrel?

FARCE MAJEURE

Feb 2, 2023

Dear Mogg
Great theory coming from my pals chez Spectator: I could run for Pres of the US! I reckon, if I did, I would smash it. Look at David Beckham - he went over there and was a brilliant basketball player for the New York Yankees. It can be done.
Generalissimo pissimo
Boris

Feb 3, 2023

Dear Raab
Things are getting a bit sweaty for you, aren't they? Now Gina Miller, eh? I'd better not say what I think about her or the wokerati will come down on me like a ton of pricks. I reckon you've got about 4 and half days left before you're given the boot.
Axit exit
Boris

Feb 3, 2023

Dear Mogg
I see that some junior whipperslacker is standing against me in my very dear constituency of Oxbridge and Ruislip. Does he really think he can match my jovial, bon vivace personality? I've stood next to a gun in Ukraine. Beat that, weed.
Caveat velocicraptor
Boris

Feb 5, 2023

Dear Mogg
I hope you caught my interview with the glorious

MICHAEL ROSEN

Nadine. I delivered my great bong mot about Captain Crasherooni Snoozefest again. Once is never enough. God I'm as good at the old lexical fireworks as Harpo Marx, don't you think?
Spandex expandix
Boris

Feb 6, 2023

Dear Mogg
In the next few months, I am foreseeing that many a lowly wretch in the Party or the Civil Service will crawl out of the woodworm and claim that under my leadership, they could do no other, thanks to me being the farce majeure.
Belarus in peru
Boris

Appointed cabinet secretary and head of the civil service by Boris Johnson, some called Simon Case the most important man in parliament whom you have never heard of.

Feb 6, 2023

Dear Mogg
My dealings with Simon Case are coming under scrutiny. I feel like Hamlet being spied on by Rosenkavalier and Guildenstone. We had parties, we had quizzes, we had fun. I stretched the truth. So what?
Drastic elastic
Boris

FARCE MAJEURE

Feb 6, 2023

Dear Mogg
See that Grant Schnapps is trying to backpedal his way over his gargantuan photo screw-up. Schnapps should learn from Macbeth: 'If it were done when it were done, then 'tis done, if 'twere quickly done, when it were done, if 'tis done.'
Thermos flasc in ascot
Boris

Feb 7, 2023

Dear Mogg
Telegraph has a terrific article on how I will surpass Winston in making a comeback. And remember Macbeth too. Even now, I see me standing at the Despatches Box, as serried ranks of pinkos opposite gasp with panic knowing defeat awaits them.
Super ego on tost
Boris

Feb 8, 2023

Dear Mogg
I'm in two minds about this politics malachi. I've just been slapped in the face with 2.5 mill smackerooni just for jetting round the US talking piffle, laced with Latin I can't remember. Why bother with wearing my botty out on the HofC benches?
Odium podium
Boris

Feb 8, 2023

Dear Mogg
When I said that I was 100% ding dang sure that Robert

MICHAEL ROSEN

Sharp knows nothing about my personal finances, I meant he knows quite a lot about my personal finances. I think that's pretty clear. As clear as the River Tiber flowing through Athens.
Quis quo quac quac quac
Boris

Reply from BoringDavid

But the River Tiber runs through...

Feb 8, 2023

Dear Mogg
In 'The Merchant of Venus', Antonio is short of readies and there have been moments in the recent past when I have been in a similar position. I deeply resent the fact that pinko MPs are crawling all over my finances.
Dipso facto
Boris

Feb 8, 2023

Dear Mogg
And they're now wheeling out Old Major! Wasn't he a character in Oscar Wilde's 'Animal Farm'? They love finding creaky old gits from the Specimen Cupboard to attack me. A suitable medication should be found for them.
Ex lax in cofi
Boris

FARCE MAJEURE

Feb 9, 2023

Dear Mogg
Cameron is a weasel. He's droning on about how the Tory interest in me is like someone in a doomed love affair. Like who? Troilus and Chrysalis? He has no deep understanding of the great tales of the past that inform our poultry lives.
Bvlgari in duodenum
Boris

Feb 9, 2023

Dear Rishi
I know that you and I have had our disagreements, mostly over the fact that you stabbed me in the back, but leaving that to one side, do you think you could find a way to asking me to partner you when you greet Mr Zolensky in future?
Escorto in doldrum
Boris

Feb 9, 2023

Dear Mogg
Well wouldn't you just know it! Sunak has stolen my thunder and done the big meet and greet with Zerinsky himself. Zerinksy is my man, not his. He's the backing singer to my solo, just as Paul Simon backed ABBA.
Candida in volvo
Boris

MICHAEL ROSEN

Feb 9, 2023

Dear Mogg
I think it's important that senior figures like you and me, make very clear that we hold Robert Sharp, head of ITV in the highest esteem. His answers at the Select Committee were of a man of great intellect and unimpeachable perspicuity.
Roget's rhinoceros
Boris

Feb 9, 2023

Dear Mogg
People ask, what does Boris do with his moolah? They have no idea of the commitments I have to fine living and the betterment of those of my family I still talk to. As Oscar Wilde said, "What do they know of England, who only England know?"
Proboscis in gelato
Boris

Feb 9, 2023

Dear Mogg
Much attention has been paid to my hair and its charming, ruffled, tousled, loose look. This renders me as endearing as Iago in 'Othello', one of Shakespeare's jolly clowns, playing the role of a joyful go-between to the lovers.
Bacchanalia failia
Boris

FARCE MAJEURE

Feb 9, 2023

Dear Mogg
People have identified me quite rightly as a hawk over the war in Ukraine. I am indeed demanding that we send Ukraine Tycoon jets to blast Putin out the sky.
Realistically, if we don't, we can expect Putin to invade Canada.
Bellicosa mucosa
Boris

Feb 9, 2023

Dear Mogg
To tell the truth (And what do I know about truth? Lols), I'm missing deadlines galore with these books I'm supposed to be writing. I don't think I've ever let anyone down before, but I sure am now. I feel like Perfidious Albert, as they say.
Mortadella con oreal
Boris

Feb 10, 2023

Dear Raab
If you were classically educated and as clever as I am, I would recommend that you should switch to giving speeches. Sadly, you're not, so there's not much else you can do but wait for the guillotine to drop as indeed it dropped on Cleopatra.
Orator per cloaca
Boris

MICHAEL ROSEN

Feb 10, 2023

Dear Nads
Do you know the Gabriel Peters song, 'Don't give up'? I feel like throwing myself in front of you and singing it to you. Think again. Remember Abba: It's our Party and we can cry if we want to.
Amor vincit insomnia
Boris

Lee Anderson was appointed Deputy Chairman of the Conservative party by Rishi Sunak. He is a controversial figure having changed parties earlier in his career and is now the MP for Ashfield in Nottinghamshire.

In a speech to Parliament he criticised those who used food banks saying that they were people who did not know how to cook or how to budget. He said that anyone could have a breakfast for 32 pence. He gave an interview to the Spectator where he said he was in favour of the death penalty being reinstated.

Feb 11, 2023

Dear Mogg
This Lee chappie who wants to hang people: of course we don't have to agree with him. The point is he's like a trawler, gathering up votes from people who get to think we'll be hanging away like billy-o when of course we won't. Hah!
Bogus marmite
Boris

FARCE MAJEURE

LXXVI

MICHAEL ROSEN

Feb 12, 2023

Dear Mogg
The media are giving Robert Sharp, head of ITV a torrid time over whether he tipped me the wink or not over where to go for some readies. The hacks are like the wild dogs that attack Baloo the panther in A.A. Milne's wonderful 'Jungle Book'.
Fanci financi
Boris

Feb 12, 2023

Dear Mogg
The actor Hugh Bonnoville has said that I am a man of no principle. Is he the guy who appeared in that dreary soap opera 'Downham Abbey'? I wish they'd bring back that marvellous Ancient Greece series with Derek Jacoby, 'Me, Claudius'.
Grippa losinga
Boris

Feb 13, 2023

Dear Stoughton and Hodder
As you're aware, progress on my great book about Shakespeare has been sluggish. I have been waylaid en croute to finishing other ventures: a global lecture tour, the war in Ukraine, and being the most famous PM since Enoch Powell.
Grovello prostate
Boris

FARCE MAJEURE

Feb 13, 2023

Dear Mogg
Glorious Telegraph saying my return is 'inevitable'. Only I can 'stop the rot', they say. As I ponder the irony, Phil Spector's words ring in my ear, 'Take a look at me now'. We will see Dickens's title, 'Return of the Native', come to pass.
Fiat lux audi lux
Boris

Posted by Shaun Wing:

Dear Boris
The great pontificator Mr Rodney Lidl told the MoS: 'It's an absurdity, an absolute absurdity, that people who might read my columns are in danger of being radicalised.' A man with a "magna lexico." Big on Verbosity, Lidl On Absurdity.
Smugg

Feb 13, 2023

O my friend
How unwise to write to the disreputable Michael Rosen. He is the Hermes to my Zeus. All queries should come to me.
Lola sho gal
Boris

Feb 14, 2023

Dear Mogg
Are you marking Valentine's Day? I muse on how we commemorate Saint Valentina with cards and flowers.

MICHAEL ROSEN

She was of course originally called Eglantina, the wild rose, which is why we give roses, but she changed her name as the Greeks often did.
Lexical aperplex
Boris

Feb 14, 2023

Dear Mogg
Now Jonathan Dimblebly is having a go at Robert Sharp, head of ITV. JD is one of the woke twatterati but does he think he's Cassandra? Well, she was cursed by the Hammersmith Apollo. No one believed her, so why believe Dimblebly?
Veritas phobia
Boris

Feb 15, 2023

Dear Mogg
With all these hints coming from the Telegraph that I'm on the way back, I'm rewriting the old Perry Cuomo song as: 'It's beginning to look a lot like Boris'. Mind you, who would have thought a governor of New York wrote the original?!
Bel canto ulcer
Boris

Feb 15, 2023

Dear Mogg
I am a genius at making pancakes. I use a tried and proven recipe from Mrs Beaten. In another life I would have been a celebrity chef along the lines of that Gordon Romsey fellow.
Sirex delia
Boris

FARCE MAJEURE

Feb 19, 2023

Dear Mogg
I see clear blue clouds between Sunak and me over this Northern Ireland Interpol agreement. I crafted it over months of painstaking work on the beach, yet his EU-leaning wets are intent on throwing it away just as King Lear rejects Desdemona.
Gol in extra tempo
Boris

Feb 19, 2023

Dear Mogg
Observer says Commons Privileged Committee (Kangaroo Court) is homing in on a supposedly illegal gathering where ABBA was being played loudly. Yes, one or two of us max were enjoying ABBA's 'Bohemian Rhapsody'. That's it. Facts are facts.
Conga in studio hic hic
Boris

Feb 19, 2023

Dear Mogg
We are desperagoes battling the woke elite who've taken over our great Party. Hacks are saying we have a 100 braves in the Parliamentary Party, ready to fight for the Union, the DUP and me, just as Oedipus fought for Caesar.
Vast deferens
Boris

Feb 20, 2023

Dear Mogg
I am weighing up whether to attend this Commons

Kangaroo Court, fully aware as I am that under cross-examination, I may come across as less affixed to the truth than Brer Hobbit was to the Tar Baby.
Trans itvan
Boris

Feb 21, 2023

Dear Billy
Please don't write to Rosen. He is nothing but a postman. I am the genius who writes these epissles.
Cava nostra
Boris

Feb 21, 2023

Dear Mogg
The Independent is running with a story of how weasel Osborne 'loathes' me. What Osborne can't stand about me is that I am someone who unites where he divides, leads where he sidelines from the carp. Cometh the man, cometh the hourglass.
Wax in orifici auditori
Boris

Feb 21, 2023

Dear Mogg
Can you remind me what political principle we're working to here? As you know, I work from the solid basis of whether it's good for Boris. It's served me well in the past. But now? I am seeing things through the grass darkly.
Principia pathologica
Boris

FARCE MAJEURE

Feb 21, 2023

Dear Mogg
In strictest confidence, you and me know that we get on fine with the jolly old DUP, don't we? They resist the EU encirclement of this sentried isle, as Shakespeare puts it so well when Prospero talks of his island in 'Twelfth Night'.
Ego in centro universo
Boris

Feb 25, 2023

Dear Mogg
As the Witches say in King Lear, 'Double trouble, double bubble'. Telegraph: 'Things 'spiralling out of control for No 10'', as a eurosceptic rebellion looms and I refuse to back the NI deal. It feels like Van Diesel and 'Here comes the night.'
Jon ursa major
Boris

Feb 25, 2023

Dear Mogg
The history of our great Unionist Party has been bolstered by what our critics have called 'playing the Orange card', a reference to us selling oranges in cardboard boxes to Ireland during the First World War. We may have to play it again.
Mona liza minelli
Boris

Feb 25, 2023

Dear Mogg
Times has labyrinthine stories re the DUP, the ERG and

me. Am I the Minotaur waiting for the Wooden Horse in the sewers of Rome then? Times says I was heard shouting 'F*** the Americans!'. Yet, I was, as Bruce Grobbelaar sang, 'Born in the USA'.
Cogito erg sum
Boris

Feb 25, 2023

Dear Mogg
This dearth in veggies bothers me in that people will say that it's a consequence of Brexit. The knock-on might then be that woke remoaning guardianista tofu-eaters will blame me - of all people! Why me?!
Aldi minus pimento
Boris

Feb 26, 2023

Dear Mogg
We need to be much more direct: 'No cap for profits. No cap for prices. Cap wages now.' If I was in Numero 10, we wouldn't be 100s of points behind the woke Trots. We need to be as bold and daring as Sir Andrew Aguecheek in 'Othello'.
Potus con nasturtium
Boris

Feb 26, 2022

Dear Mogg
Are you locked in secret talks with Mark Francois? I have to seriously consider whether I should tie my laces to any star steered by Francois. Death by contact is a political truth. Never jump till the last dog barks.
Dilemma bona fido
Boris

FARCE MAJEURE

"Rishi Sunak snubs Boris Johnson over new Brexit deal
PM faces revolt as minister 'on resignation watch' after being shut out of negotiations"

The Telegraph - Feb 25, 2023

Feb 26, 2023

Dear Mogg
Is Sunak going to pull off this NI deal and am I going to be left with face on my egg looking like I was as opposed to a settlement as Julius Caesar was at the Treaty of Versailles? Which way do your trousers hang on this one?
Picasso in costco
Boris

Feb 27, 2023

Dear Mogg
We need to get in a huddle and talk chicken. The turkeys are coming home to roost and if we play our carts right, we could topple Sunak. We have to look reasonable whilst being obdurate bastards.
Ultimatum patum pepperum
Boris

Feb 28, 2023

Dear Mogg
I'm engaged in discussions with the DUP. They propped up May's government for a few months so it'll be appropriate for them to give me a leg-up too. I'm told that shouting 'Erin go bragh' at the end of the meeting will go down well with them.

MICHAEL ROSEN

Dulux in burrito
Boris

Feb 28, 2023

Dear Mogg
If this NI deal goes through I'm snookered with this touch down in the last minute. My first feeling is that we should torpedo it in the boatswain. Then I will emerge like Nero from the Wooden Horse to seize the victor decorum.
Elastico opportunistico
Boris

Newspapers and news programmes are all reporting on Rishi Sunak's deal with the EU over Northern Ireland called the Windsor Framework.

Rishi Sunak has said his new Brexit deal puts Northern Ireland in a 'unbelievably special position' because it gives the nation access to both the UK and European Union markets - making it the 'world's most exciting economic zone.'

It is reported that the Prime Minister told firms they should 'take advantage of Northern Ireland's very special position.'

Feb 28, 2023

Dear Mogg
The great Roman philosopher Confucius said that even the longest journey starts not with a bang but a whimper. So it is that we will cunningly deflate the planks of Sunak's springboard.
Baldric in talcum
Boris

FARCE MAJEURE

Mar 1, 2023

Dear Mogg
Worrying times. The window of opportunity seems to be levering towards an undesirable impasse and as Lady Macbeth says, 'O my oblivion is a very Antony and I am all forgotten'.
Dumbo con salsa trans orient espresso
Boris

"Matt Hancock claims 'doctored' WhatsApp leak 'fits anti-lockdown agenda'
The Telegraph has obtained more than 100,000 messages from Whitehall during the Covid crisis"

The Telegraph - 1 Mar, 2023

Isabel Oakshott, a writer and journalist, caused an uproar in Westminster. She had ghost written Matt Hancock's memoir. He had trusted her with his WhatsApp Messages that took place during the period of the pandemic when there was a countrywide lockdown. The memoir came out in December. Although, as a ghost writer she was in a trusted position, nevertheless, she took these messages to The Daily Telegraph who, of course, published some; her excuse for her actions was that she wanted the world to know the truth about decisions made about lockdown of which she was a fierce critic.

The former health secretary Matt Hancock has repeatedly criticised the leaks, referring to the published messages as a 'partial, biased account to suit an anti-lockdown agenda.'

Mar 1, 2023

Dear Mogg
The Times is saying that these leaks show that I said that the risk from Covid was 'no worse than falling

downstairs'. I don't know whether I said that. I don't know if I didn't say that. Did Romeo know that he had killed Malvolio?
Rhetorical bolux
Boris

Mar 1, 2023

Dear Matt Talkcock
Your cook is goosed. This latest revelation makes you a rogue elephant, defeated in battle, cast out, trumpeting hopelessly across the savannah, roaming the wilderness, never to return again. Don't ask how I know.
Glorioso multi kanga testiculo
Boris

Mar 2, 2023

Dear Mogg
The great thing about 'taking back control' was that it meant less power for Europe and more power for me. Tragically, not for me right now, though. But there is a time for everything, as it says in Enclosiastes in the Bible.
Ulterior motor
Boris

Mar 2, 2023

Dear Mogg
My speech today was superb. I have told the world that this NI so-called 'deal', is not Brexitty enough. The people of NI will still be under the heel of the global grasp of the north London woke tofu-eating elite.
Neon gorgonzola in pancreas
Boris

FARCE MAJEURE

Mar 2, 2023

Dear Mogg
My thoughts range over prisons deep and cold enough for the frightful Oakeshott to be cast into. Perhaps the one portrayed in Victor Hugo's 'The Count of Monte Crispo'. Deeds leading to mistrust of politicians must be punished.
Ex bisto in spandex
Boris

Mar 2, 2023

Dear Mogg
I feel the reins of power slipping from my grasp just as, in the Bible, the reins slip from the grasp of Ben Nevis in the great chariot race, as seen in the film where Ben Nevis was played by Charlton Heston Services.
Inebrio con brio
Boris

Mar 2, 2023

Dear Mogg
I am steaming over this attempt by Labour to give the awful Sue Gray some top post. It undermines the civil service. That's our job. We've been doing it for years. Reminds me of that ABBA song 'Should have been me'.
Cosi fan totti
Boris

Mar 3, 2023

Dear Mogg
Did you see the screen behind me as I spoke yesterday? It said, 'Global Soft Power'. Global - me - yes. Power - me - yes. Soft? Me? Not! I am the iron glove in wolf's

clothing. I slammed the police for fining me for having lunch. That told'em.
Rumbaba in limbo
Boris

Mar 3, 2023

Dear Mogg
I'm taking on board some much needed liquid refreshment while trying to understand why Hanshott and Oakcock are about to lock corns over this matter of who said what. Do we know what Napoleon said to Churchill?
Quis quo quiche
Boris

Mar 3, 2023

Dear Mogg
The Kangaroo Court has published a squalid interim report. It's clearly an attempt to prejudice the matter with sub jure de facto ex officio insomnia. You will stand by me, Moggo? Just as Plato stood by Horatio on the bridge over the River Kwai.
Kinetic ex lax
Boris

Mar 4, 2023

Dear Mogg
The nation is quivering in anticipation on a cliff-wedge like an oven-ready drag anchor awaiting my revelation of who is on my honours list. I won't disappoint. People will welcome my choice just as the nation swept Churchill to power in 1945.
Renta gobbo
Boris

FARCE MAJEURE

Mar 4, 2023

Dear Nadine
Every time I read your supportive words about me in the press, I'm reminded of that great Ben E. Hill song, 'Stand by me'. And, you won't know this, but when he was betrayed, 'twas only Cleopatra who stood by Erasmus.
Myxomatosis in celeriac
Boris

Mar 4, 2023

Dear Mogg
Weasels and backstabbers have snitched on me to the Kangaroo Court. Hah! They'll never prove that I 'deliberately' misled the House because I will say that I 'mistakenly' misled the House. Did Orsino recognise that Cesario was really Desdemona?
Esso phobia
Boris

Mar 5, 2023

Dear Mogg
I sense that vastly incriminating info will emerge from this cash of WhatZap messages that Annabel Oakeshott has released. Sunak will go down like a bled lagoon. Remember the Zeppelins shot down in the Crimean War, Moggo.
Peston super Mare
Boris

Mar 5, 2023

Dear Mogg
If Starmer takes on disloyal Sue Gray, we'll see him for what he is: a raving Stalinist woke Trot, up to his eyes in

tofu and asylum-seekers. I will be exonerated in the face of vicious vituperation. I stand on the blink of a heroic return.
Toblerone in rectum
Boris

Mar 5, 2023

Dear Mogg
I'm getting emails from disloyal woke wets in our Party urging me to cease my mental feet to restore my reputation and rightful pinnacle at the peak of Party, Government and Country. As Jarvis Bieber sang, 'I'm the one'.
Intestate nasturtium non durex
Boris

Chris Heaton-Harris is the MP for Daventry. He has been serving as Secretary of State for Northern Ireland since the 6th September, appointed by Liz Truss.

Mar 5, 2023

Dear Mogg
Good old Chris Harris-Heaton. He's been talking to Laura K., backing me up as not knowingly misleading the House over Partygate. Warriors loyal to their king is what I need right now, just as Oedipus and Virgil were loyal to Hannibal.
Spasmodic ricotta
Boris

FARCE MAJEURE

Mar 5, 2023

Dear Mogg
My old pal Tom Bristow, MP for Peterborough says on Sky quite rightly that the so-called 'party' was just soggy sandwiches and a slice of cake. Exactly! Sue Gray totally failed to keep the sandwiches fresh and there was no bloomin' Beluga.
Bogus persil in plasma
Boris

Mar 5, 2023

Dear Mogg
The Telegraph has pounced on the leaks saying they show that I veered from lockdown sceptic to lockdown zealot. I deny that I was ever a septic. Cynic perhaps - along the lines of the great Greek philosopher Galileo.
Persona non gratin
Boris

Mar 5, 2023

Dear Mogg
Chris Harris-Heaton Harris says that he believes I'm an honest man. Hah! Probably the last man standing who does believe it, but I'll take that. Take That! Maybe I should get Ronan Keating from that band to show his support for me.
Tobasco erotica
Boris

Mar 6, 2023

Dear Mogg
Do you think I could wangle it so that my two nippers

could get on to my honours' list? A bit like being put down for Eton when you're a kid but it's for an honour instead - a kind of delayed peerage. Can't think why not.
Superior urticaria
Boris

Mar 7, 2023

Dear Mogg
I did nothing wrong! You and Nadine and my last loyal followers need to spell it out to the idiot populace: I was sandbagged by woke lefties camelflaged as Tories just as Juliet wore a mask to get into the Montagus' party.
Vindolanda vindalu
Boris

Mar 7, 2023

Dear Mogg
People are trying to interfere with my sanctified right to give an honour to my great father. They will fail as do all who hurl lances against me. Achilles may have had an Achilles' Hole in his knee but before that, he, like me, was invincible.
Mythos mathmos
Boris

Mar 7, 2023

Dear Mogg
I'm watching which way opinion is going on this asylum seeker story. If it looks as if the glorious Suella has got it right, I shall come up with something yet more dragonian. If opinion is against, I'll be ruthless in my condemnation. I am a leader.
Pox vops
Boris

FARCE MAJEURE

Mar 7, 2023

Dear Mogg
Suella has a new term - 'an activist blob' of 'left-wing lawyers, civil servants and the Labour Party' who've 'blocked us'. Does this go far enough? Why not include 'cultural Marxists', 'north London metropolitan elite' and 'teachers who hate work'?
Mega vacuum
Boris

Meanwhile on Twitter, Gary Lineker, the presenter of Match of the Day on the BBC, has tweeted that the language being used by Conservative Ministers is 'not dissimilar to that used by Germany in the 30s'. The government has protested and demanded he be suspended for not reflecting the BBC's policy of political impartiality.

He tweeted that in his opinion: 'There is no huge influx. We take far fewer refugees than other major European countries.'

Mar 8, 2023

Dear Mogg
It has been revealed that I have given evidence to the committee investigating Dominic Rab. Some are querying why I have done this. It's because I am a trustworthy and reliable witness just as Iago is in 'Hamlet'.
Tandoori non balti
Boris

Mar 9, 2023

Dear Mogg
Again, the hacks tedious chatter broadcast to the world details of my hard-earned income. Yes, £4 mill so far

MICHAEL ROSEN

this year. While traitors sought to cut me down, the market values my true worth. I'm so golden, as Harry Belafonte sang.
Moola in tutti orifici
Boris

Mar 11, 2023

Dear Mogg
I think we're in a terrific place as regards the BBC. We want to close the damn thing down (obvs), and having our chaps in key jobs inside, means they can pull the whole thing down for us just as Samsung pulled down the temple.
Conga wonga
Boris

Michael Rosen replied:

I don't often edit Boris Johnson's letters, but I'm now of the opinion that Wonga conga would have been a better sign off.

BBC Report: Stars walk out in solidarity after Lineker suspended. Gary Lineker was suspended by the BBC when he refused to apologise for comparing the language used by government ministers in regard to refugees with that of Germany in the 1930s. Then ex-England footballers, Alan Shearer and Ian Wright and also presenters Alex Scott and Jason Mohammad refused to take over Lineker's role.

FARCE MAJEURE

Mar 11, 2023

Dear Mogg
This frightful action being taken by BBC sports staff is a wildcat strike and one of the marvellous things that Margaret did was to outlaw such action. If only I were PM now! I'd be singing out this truth just as Feste does in 'King Lear'.
Phi beta crappa
Boris

Mar 11, 2023

Dear Mogg
Sunak is dithering. I would be decisive. It's been pointed out to me that Lord Sugar is something of an expert on soccer and he's impartial. Thus I have a solution to the present impasto: Sugar to present Matches of the Day.
Intra venus harpic
Boris

Mar 11, 2023

Dear Mogg
I sense that the BBC's move against Garry Linacre is beginning to harm us. He was a great soccer player, one of England's best ever defenders. The problem with the BBC suspending him is that he looks like as much of a martyr as I am.
Vivat bex
Boris

Mar 12, 2023

Dear Mogg
One way out of this Linacre debackle is to not only shorten Matches of the Day but also to shorten the

soccer matches. Less soccer, less commentating, less Linacre. I will talk to friends.
Gladiolus in pastrami
Boris

Mar 12, 2023

Dear Mogg
One obvious way out of this Linneker stand-off is to ask him to make a substantial donation to the Conservative Party. This will prove that he's impartial. Another of my great ideas. 'Take a chance on me', as Boyzone sang.
Bento box bossa nova
Boris

Mar 13, 2023

Dear Mogg
Seen your comment that the BBC licence fee is past its sell-by date. Yes! We have to allow the market to let rip with turbo-charged entrepreneurial peppa-piggery. Even when we stuff their boardroom with trusties, they go native and go woke.
Torpedo in tofu
Boris

Mar 14, 2023

Dear Mogg
I admire Suella. She has a way with words for our enemies: cultural Marxists, wokerati, tofu-eaters, Guardian readers, billions of migrants, migrants connected to drugs. Do you think she means that tofu is one of the drugs?
Gastro pandemonium
Boris

FARCE MAJEURE

Craig MacKinley was a very active member of UKIP for several years. He joined the Conservative party in 2005 and was, of course, a strong Brexit supporter. He was born in Chatham and is keen on sailing. However, his popularity has begun to wane because Kent has suffered from very hot summers and as he is a cimate change denier he has voted against measures to tackle climate change.

Mar 14, 2023

Dear Mogg
I agree with Craig MacKinlay MP for Thinnit or Thanet or somewhere. He's worried that the BBC has given Liniker a carte blanche to say what he wants. This country is in a bad place if it allows someone to say what he wants.
Capaldi in avocado
Boris

The Foundation Philosophy

While on this plane Chief Anyiam-Osigwe adopted and propagated an approach to existence which is premised on the universality of Truth, and emphasized the harmony that exists in the teachings of such great masters as Christ, Mohammed, Buddha and Confucius.

March 14th, 2023 - Information:

1) Mr [Boris] Johnson...will bring to bear his experiential knowledge as one of the significant international statesmen of the 21st century to examine the central theme of the lecture, 'Rehumanising Human Experience: A Synopsis of Anyiam-Osigwe's treatises.'

2) The former Mayor of London and former UK Foreign Secretary, through his keynote address, will offer solutions to some of the global challenges that are currently plaguing the

world, stoking citizens' frustrations and anger, the statement noted.

Mar 14, 2023

Dear Mogg
Don't laugh, but I'm giving lectures on 'rehumanizing human experience' and 'offering solutions to global challenges'!!! Do people really think I know anything at all about this stuff?! No matter: I am the Knossos of Rhodes and can do anything.
Impromptu bunkum
Boris

Mar 15, 2023

Dear Mogg
Have you seen what the adorable Priti has said? The investigation into me will 'put our democracy in a very, very bad light'. Indeed! As Jaundice and Jaundice might say, 'the law is not above the law, the law is the law.'
Calypso facto
Boris

Mar 17, 2023

Dear Mogg
Glorious vote of confidence from my constituency party in Oxbridge and Riuslip - I am reselected, just as the tribunes of Athens chose Nero. Ringing in my eyes are the memorable words that Malvolio says to Prospero: 'This island's mine.'
Tequila in cerebrum
Boris

FARCE MAJEURE

Martin Forde KC was appointed by Keir Starmer to undertake an independent inquiry into the circumstances of the labour party's own inquiry into antisemitism. The report was published in 2022.

Mar 17, 2023

Dear Mogg
I muse upon the latest from Martin Forde KC. There are times in politics, Moggo, when, 'tis best for the likes of us if the clamour be stilled; better to be ignored than adored. Bruce Springsteen's 'The Sound of Silence' says it all.
Camera obskewer
Boris

Mar 18, 2023

Dear Mogg
I think we should start being more pliable over Brexit. Should it turn out that it hasn't been quite the success that we predicted, we must consider jumping horses, switching ship, and becoming a pro-EU faction, with me at the helmet.
Vivat flex
Boris

Mar 18, 2023

Dear Mogg
One of the reasons why I admire the splendid Suella is that she is so willing to tear up all the musty old principles and red tape of the legal system. We know people are doing bad stuff, so why try them? Let's just label them 'illegal'.
Crap diem
Boris

MICHAEL ROSEN

Mar 19, 2023

Dear Mogg
I've assembled an unbeatable team to win out against the Kangaroo Court coming up. I will use the great Blair defence: I didn't ***knowingly*** mislead the house even if I did mislead them. Gettit? They can't read my mind any more than I can.
Lordi panic buton
Boris

Mar 19, 2023

Dear Mogg
Only tofu-eating lefty lawyers stand between brave Suella and getting the great Rwanda bill over the line. I hate lawyers - apart from Lord Panic who will win for me this week. I will cross the Rubicon, like Caesar at the Battle of the Bulge.
Quasi stasi
Boris

Mar 19, 2023

Dear Mogg
I'm all over the Sundays as they speculate on how I will fare at the Kangaroo Court this week. Lo how they write my political obituary, little knowing that I have many a trump card to play. I'm reminded of that old Dick of Cards recitation.
Intra venus tex rita
Boris

FARCE MAJEURE

Mar 19, 2023

Dear Mogg
Good old Kwesi Kwarteng. He says I will win at the Kangaroo Court and become the leader again. You see? Some people are faithful and rally round the Great One, just as Iago supported Othello. I'm minded of Tommy Wynette's 'Stand by your Man'.
Lego in paella
Boris

There was a video leaked to the press in December 2021 of Allegra Stratton, a newly appointed government spokesperson, jokingly referring to Christmas Parties in Number 10 Downing Street. Of course, she lost her job. It is seen as an example of how, led by Boris Johnson, no one behaved responsibly in Downing Street.

Mar 20, 2023

Dear Mogg
The play-acting of the delightful Allegra is being harnessed in order to find me guilty before trial by the Kangaroo Court. O ye of little froth, know ye not Hamlet: 'the play's the thing, wherein I'll crunch the concrete of the king'?
Austin allegro non cortina
Boris

MICHAEL ROSEN

Mar 20, 2023

Dear Mogg
Judicious leaking to the Telegraph reveals our tactics for the forthcoming Kangaroo Court. We will outlaw the bolshevik, Stalinist, Trot, cultural Marxist, Guardian-reading, tofu-eating wokerati on the committee before they open their gobs.
Sub judice dench
Boris

Mar 20, 2023

Dear Mogg
This Lee Anderson chap is quite a cove. What do you make of his idea of getting prisoners to pick fruit? I guess one of the probs with that would be how to stop them running away. We should never forget that great movie, Shawshank Reduction.
Sudafed in macaroni
Boris

Mar 20, 2023

Dear Mogg
My stupendous, bombshell 50 page report is in with the Kangaroo Court. It will blow them away like a lead balloon. Lord Panic shows that the whole basis of this committee will crumble like crumble.
Hobo sapiens
Boris

"Boris' Partygate evidence was delayed because it had a 'number of errors and typos'"

Metro - Mar 21, 2023

FARCE MAJEURE

In the 52 pages of the document, the former prime minister admitted he did mislead parliament but denied he did so knowingly.

The Committee of Privileges has revealed that the initial unredacted evidence package that was handed in on Monday afternoon included mistakes.

A 'final corrected version' was not submitted until 8.02am on Tuesday morning, they said – only 30 hours before the hearing is due to start.

Questioned on the claims, a source close to Mr Johnson admitted: 'There were a small number of cosmetic changes to the typing.'

MPs on the committee have also revealed that the written submission contains 'no new documentary evidence'.

Mar 21, 2023

Dear Mogg
More effort is needed by my loyal followers to rubbish the Privileged Committee trying me on Weds. Only when a chorus of rage and derision washes over them like the rock of ages, will I leap free of the manacles that bind my weary brow.
Extra curricula hyperbole
Boris

Mar 21, 2023

Dear Mogg
We're teetering on the rink. Just 2 days to go before what will be my stunning appearance before the world. I will sweep aside the lefty lawyers and woke stooges who seek revenge on the greatest prime minister since Enoch Powell.
In pantechnicon ad dopamine
Boris

MICHAEL ROSEN

Mar 21, 2023

Dear Mogg
It's really quite simple: I knew my parties broke the rules but when I told the House I wasn't at the parties, I did so in good faith. Trouble is, people don't understand that I'm saying that I lied honestly.
Panacea mega duplicito
Boris

Mar 21, 2023

Dear Mogg
At last the world can see my honesty for what it is. The pillow holding up my defence is, 'how could I have known that we were breaking the rules? All the other folks enjoying the jollies, didn't say, 'Stop!', did they?
Alibi baba
Boris

Mar 21, 2023

Dear Mogg
My defence is 'how could I have known the parties were breaking the rules?' Must have been the same for everyone else in the country. They just didn't know if they were breaking the rules.
Semolina ad astra
Boris

FARCE MAJEURE

Mar 22, 2023

Dear Mogg
The hair is washed to render it endearingly tousled, and I will show the world my masterful oratory while my interrogators become mired in hesitant blather. I will shine like bright metal on dull ground, as Prince Hal says in The Tempest.
Bolax in extremis
Boris

Mar 22, 2023

Dear Mogg
What these clodhopping interrogators don't get is that when there are regs and guidelines, it doesn't mean that they have to be stuck to exactly in some crazy totalitarian way. The Romans may have built the Parthenon but they didn't do it rigidly.
Pro bolli
Boris

Brian Walker replied:

So unrigidly that they were 5 BCE Greeks not Romans

Mar 22, 2023

Dear Brian
If you look closely, you'll see that this missive comes from me, Boris, not from that irritating ignoranus, Michael Rosen. You should address your criticisms to me.
Protozoa in pesto
Boris

Michael Rosen wrote:

I was in hospital in 2020. @underthcranes (Emma) and the children couldn't come in to see me from Mar 28 till mid-May when (special conditions) they wheeled me into the atrium so she could help wake me up from the coma. I'm delighted Johnson and pals were partying at the time.

Lynn Hilman-fox replied:

In the April 2020 we had to wear three layers of PPE to help our daughter wake up from a coma. We were then not allowed to visit her. I could not see Mum in the care home December 2020, and she died in that same home Jan 21. So pleased Boris was enjoying himself!

Mar 22, 2023

Dear Mogg
How am I doing? Aren't I brilliant? I parry their feeble skewers just as Tybalt fought off Romeo. There is now no way this Privileged Committee can find me guilty any more than the courts ever found Jeffrey Archer guilty.
Mendacius pepsi max
Boris

Mar 22, 2023

Dear Mogg
How could I have known what the rules were? Who was responsible for them anyway? Little moles beavering away in the basement of the Commons come up with this stuff and expect a great statesman like me to comply. Pah!
Non conscius pro blotto
Boris

FARCE MAJEURE

> "Harman's face was thunder. Boris was as agile as a cat. Pure box office but, after four nit-picking hours, had a single mind been changed?"

Mail Online - Mar 23, 2023

Sarah Vine reviews ex-PM's battle to clear his name and salvage his career over Partygate. She calls him 'The Captain Jack Sparrow of British politics, buccaneer and charming rogue', while those speaking for the privileges committee are 'slow and ponderous'.

Mar 22, 2023

Dear Mogg
If they believe this stuff, they're more bonkers than me. Of course, I knew the jollies were against the regs! How could I not know they were, so when I misled the House, I knew I had! Anyway, last throw of the lice!
Baloni in excesso
Boris

Mar 22, 2023

Dear Mogg
Not one of that wretched committee made the point that the reason I didn't know it was a party was because I was smashed. Hah bloody hah.
In spiritu sanctu plonctu
Boris

MICHAEL ROSEN

Mar 23, 2023

Dear Mogg
I'm indebted to the redoubtable Lord Greenhalgh on Newsnight tonight. What a fine fellow: sincere, eloquent and honest. I couldn't want for a more stalwart defender. His appearance on the show tonight will greatly further our cause.
Gloria in excelsis meo
Boris

Mar 23, 2023

Dear Mogg
People have noticed my erstwhile legal representative, Lord Panic, sat behind me during marsupial proceedings yesterday and appeared to be disapprovingly raising eyebrows at key points in my brilliant defence. Who does he think he is? Rumbole?
In iambic gasometer
Boris

Mar 23, 2023

Dear Mogg
I hope the delicious Sarah Vine starts up 'Boris Johnson is innocent OK'. I want to see it painted up on bridges, opera houses and on the sides of buses where all good slogans get put. The people will shower palms beneath my feet and cry Bandanna!
Motto in grotto
Boris

FARCE MAJEURE

Mar 23, 2023

Dear Mogg
Look, if you can't have a piss-up every time someone leaves, what's the point of going on? Is it necessary for work, as the rules required? I don't know but it was certainly bloody good fun. And that's the main point.
Saturnalia vomitarium
Boris

Mar 23, 2023

Dear Mogg
One day, when Britain is in danger, King Arthur will wake from his sleep and save the nation. This will be me. They may still my powers now but there will come a time when this Silurian legend will play out.
Excalibur non sequitur
Boris

Mar 23, 2023

Dear Mogg
You're absolutely right! Yesterday was the revenge of the remainiacs. They were just after Brexitty blood and in their eyes I'm the main culprit. Clearly, Bernard Jenkins has switched to being a remaniac just as Peppa Pig became Paddington Bear.
Ramona lisa kudro
Boris

MICHAEL ROSEN

Mar 23, 2023

Dear Mogg
Ultimately, that committee don't know what I knew and what I didn't know. In fact no one knows what I knew and what I didn't know and my whole point is that I didn't know what I knew and what I didn't know which is why I was a great PM.
In post mortem miasma
Boris

Mar 23, 2023

Dear Mogg
We're getting to a good place: if the marsupial tribunal find me guilty, we will slam back at them with a bombshell torpedo napalm gun, telling them that we do not accept their piffling judgement. I am like Romeo who refused to be banished.
Surplus hubris on patio
Boris

Mar 26, 2023

Dear Mogg
Keep this under your hair: our plan is to squeeze the four Tories on the Marsupial Committee so hard that they resign. Then the whole edifice will crumble just as it crumbled when Delilah pulled down the Temple on top of Samson.
Cannabis in bognor regis
Boris

FARCE MAJEURE

MICHAEL ROSEN

Mar 27, 2023

Dear Mogg
The news is out: "The Osigwe Anyiam-Osigwe Foundation has invited Boris Johnson to share perspectives on how to promote love and peace in Lagos." I'll tell'em how I'm inspired by Troilus and Candida.
Amor et pax et banca banca banca
Boris

Mar 29, 2023

Dear Mogg
As part of my lucrative Lagos trip, I socked it to 'em about Partygate. 'Fined for eating lunch at my desk', I said. Slightly clashes with your 'fined for eating cake' but this adds to my jovial Falstaffian persona, so much loved in 'Twelfth Night'.
Payola perpetua
Boris

Mar 29, 2023

Dear Mogg
The Teleg is covering this fantastic initiative you and the gorgeous Nadine have set up, Conservative Democractic Organisation to 'take back control' of our great Party. Am slightly concerned that this sounds a little like a coup d'attack.
Ocado in bere regis
Boris

FARCE MAJEURE

Mar 29, 2023

Dear Mogg
They're editing Agatha Christie's romcoms. Sales of my great novel 'Fifty-eight Virgins' are down, due to wokerati objecting to my robust portrayal of Jews and Arabs. Editing may be the answer, just as Shakespeare was edited by Galileo.
Solar plexus penne rigate
Boris

Mar 29, 2023

Dear Mogg
There's an irritating obsession with the truth. Why do trivia-riven press hacks and lowlife backbench MPs devote so much attention to the tiny details but miss the big picture - which is me? In truth, I am the elephant in the tomb.
Quando quando quando
Boris

Mar 29, 2023

Dear Constituents of Oxbridge and Riuslip
You may have seen reports in the press castigating me for my lecturing tour. I wish to remind you that your concerns are at all times uppermost in my heart and mind just as Socrates always remembered Julius Caesar.
Trex in memoriam
Boris

MICHAEL ROSEN

Mar 30, 2023

Dear Mogg
Remember, I won the Red Wall! With the 3 words, 'Get Brexit Done', I grabbed the ancient socialist fiefdoms, as Caesar grabbed Ecuador. The northern Visigoths are deserting smoothie Sunak and only me and my ruffled hair can hang on to them.
Yamaha minus petunia
Boris

Mar 31, 2023

Dear Mogg
The FT latest on me is I'm supposedly 'like an ITV3 re-run'. Hah bloody hah. They think they're some bloomin' satirical jester like Feste in 'The Tempest'. Just wait and see, FT hack, I will rise like the Felix from the ashes of the Sunak govt.
Bombastic halitosis
Boris

Mar 31, 2023

Dear Mogg
I'm weighing the sods of me losing this Marsupial Court verdict. Probs best thing to do is accept humbly like Uriah Heap in 'Great Expectations', and that way might avoid byelection in my beloved constituency of Oxbridge and Riuslip.
Dodo salami in metro
Boris

FARCE MAJEURE

Apr 1, 2023

Dear Mogg
The frightful Newsnight have sleuthed out why my Honours List has been delayed: obsessive little bureaucrats have been vetting my choices and find some of them suspect. Solution: sack the bureaucrats - just as Churchill fired Disraeli.
Mars twix aero
Boris

Those responsible for choosing the UK entrant for Eurovision in 2023 chose a young singer called Mae Muller. It was announced in mid-March. A lively but not very well-known singer, she made it clear she supported the striking nurses and doctors.

Apr 1, 2023

Dear Mogg
Horrified! Telegraph says our entrant for Eurovision is some woke leftie called Max Miller who's attacked me. This is like Spartacus leading the slave uprising, as played by Douglas Adams in the film. I say, 'Stop Max Miller Now'.
Prix in gazebo
Boris

Apr 2, 2023

Dear Mogg
As the rust settles and we start to see the good from the trees, we need to build up a bed of steam in support of sensible voices like Suella, Nadine and me. She's talking intelligently about Rwanda, Pakistani men and white English girls.

MICHAEL ROSEN

Audio trauma sodium
Boris

Apr 2, 2023

Dear Mogg
The English Channel is English. Tragically, Caesar was unable to bring the great Roman civilisation across the Channel here so we were barbaric for many more years, just as I am being thwarted from bringing civilisation to the English too.
Peri peri in cloaca
Boris

Apr 2, 2023

Dear Mogg
I need to get on this small boat bandwaggon asap. Suella has shown how the fate of the NHS, Education, housing, street safety, teenage health all rest on us stopping them. I'll go and stand on Dover Beach and wave a flag.
Pro patria in pitta
Boris

Apr 2, 2023

Dear Mogg
I am loving Suella sticking to her gums. Laura K says to her that there's evidence of refugees being killed in Rwanda. Suella says Rwanda is safe. She is like Stonewall Jackson Pollock, the Civil War General. Send Albanians to Rwanda now!
Wacco serco
Boris

FARCE MAJEURE

CXVIII

MICHAEL ROSEN

Apr 2, 2023

Dear Mogg
Am preparing my next speech: "When Elgar wrote his great poem 'Dover Beach', how little could he have predicted how soon it would be swarming with billions of Albanians..." How am I doing?
Elegiac bolax
Boris

Clovis@Beecharmer56 replied:

Didn't Matthew Arnold write Dover Beach, or is there another Dover Beach I don't know about?!

Apr 2, 2023

Dear Clovis
It disturbs me that you have addressed this tweet to the fraud Michael Rosen. I am the sole writer of these missives and I am 100% correct in all of them.
Damson et Delilah
Boris

Apr 3, 2023

Dear Mogg
The cheek of it! George Osborne has put out a statement that there is no prospect I'll be PM again. Osborne was just the kind of weed we used to debag at Eton. That's why his job now is running Madame Tussaud's.
Paella in mascara
Boris

FARCE MAJEURE

Apr 8, 2023

Dear Mogg
Good man this Dan Wotton guy. He's linked the US establishment's persecution of Trump with the UK establishment's persecution of me. Same way we see in Twelfth Night, Toby Belch and Feste persecute Mercutio.
Bandanna in excelsis deo
Boris

Keith Flett replied:

Belch was right to persecute Mercurio. Boris is misremembering here.

Apr 8, 2023

Dear Flett
Your letters reveal to the world that you are atofu-eating, woke, bearded Guardian letter-writer. Mercurio is in 'Hamlet'. Malvolio is in 'Romeo and Juliet' and Mercutio is in 'Othello' and Othello is in 'The Tempest'.
Bono in abba
Boris

Apr 9, 2023

Dear Mogg
Have you received your invite for the Coro? We have. What a perfect day for showing the Great British People that I am Britain's number one statesman. it will be clear that Sunak is the usurper.
Caesar salata in tesco
Boris

MICHAEL ROSEN

Apr 10, 2023

Dear Mogg
Whose side is the Teleg on? They say I didn't scrutinise the HS3 project carefully enough. Poppycods! I pored over the plans for every line, every cutting, every tunnel. Mole from the Winnie the Pooh books couldn't have studied tunnels more.
De profundis londis
Boris

Apr 13, 2023

Dear Mogg
The hacks have spotted that my old and very safe seat of Henley has become vacant and are speculating that I might nip across to there from my constituency of Oxbridge and Riuslip just as Romeo moves from Verona to Paris.
Chorizo in extremis
Boris

Apr 14, 2023

Dear Mogg
I feel the time leading up to the Marsupials' judgement, weighing on me heavily. As Shakespeare put it so beautifully: "Like as the waves make towards the pebble dash, so do our minutes hasten to their end."
Tempus fuxit
Boris

FARCE MAJEURE

Apr 15, 2023

Dear Mogg
Some Tory local election leaflets have pics of me on them. What does this tell you? That I am treasured deep in the hearts of the Great British People, like the treasure in Robert Lewis Capaldi's 'Treasure Island'. X marks the pot, eh?
Hispaniola guardiola
Boris

Toby White replied:

I'm missing something here, why Capaldi and not Stevenson?

Apr 15, 2023

Dear Toby
All correspondence should be addressed to me, Boris, not to the charlatan and weasel, Michael Rosen. I am the sole writer of these missives.
Cicero in latrina
Boris

Shaun Wing wrote:

Dear Boris
The hero is Your good self. I recall Malcom X who told his 'MPeople;' "you've got to search for the hero inside yourself... search for the "occulta abscondis."" And there is the key & the secret + Grassbrute Tories know this via the teachings of Gabriel.
Smugg

MICHAEL ROSEN

Apr 17, 2023

Dear Mogg
Have fastened on to the London traffic wotsit and this Ulay thing. We're saying that the Digestion Zone is big enough. Am hoping it's going to be a national issue propelling me into the linelight again before the Marsupials get their teeth into me.
Mondeo in mayo
Boris

Apr 18, 2023

Dear Mogg
The Party Chairman has been quoted as saying that I could be ideal for leading the hustings, charging the soap box in these local elections in June. I could be the panacea, the placebo, the bazooka that steadies the ship with banners aloof.
Torpedo in speedos
Boris

April 21, 2023

Dear Mogg
I see that the excessively junior Dowden has climbed the greasy pole. I feel like Macbeth who saw that standing in the way of him winning the crown, stood Bianco.
However, good news: he's handicapped by being state educated.
Superior posterior
Boris

"Dominic Raab quits as report criticises his 'unreasonably aggressive conduct'"

The Guardian - Apr 21, 2023

FARCE MAJEURE

The Deputy Prime Minister and Justice Secretary resigns after an inquiry into bullying allegations finds he was 'intimidating' towards civil servants.

Apr 21, 2023

Dear Mogg
To see the beastly Raab depart the scene cheers me up no end. Yes, I am experiencing a bout of sharpenfreude to see one of those who conspired against me get his comeuppants, just as Oberon is slain by Bottom.
Tosca wilde
Boris

Apr 21, 2023

Dear Raab
And so you go. You are, just as Ella Fitzgerald was one too, Destiny's Child. How right you are, in the words of Bob Dylan, 'to rage against the night, rage against the conspiracy against you, against me, against truth, against a good sherry.'
Brasso in colon
Boris

Apr 21, 2023

Dear Mogg
My o my, Raab is certainly punching back today, isn't he? In fact, he's punching back so hard, it's getting clearer and clearer as to why he's been given the shove! Self-incrimination or what, eh Moggo?
Portico pugilistico
Boris

MICHAEL ROSEN

Apr 21, 2023

Dear Raab
Am watching your destiny playing out like the entrails of a goblet on the tapestry of the divine. As Beethoven said, 'Politics is the art of the passable.' You, (like me), await judgement by those lesser than us. Needs must. Needs mustard.
Impromptu antirrhinum
Boris

Apr 22, 2023

Dear Raab
I hate to crow but the bitter fruit you are forced to consume is that you tried to curb the powers of lawyers but in the end it was a lawyer who brought about your waterfall. But then you were one of the backstabbers.
Vista la hasta
Boris

"'I'm the Führer, the king': inside Boris Johnson's chaotic world"

The Times - April 22, 2023

The article contained extracts from 'Johnson at 10: The Inside Story' by Anthony Seldon and Raymond Newell. One quote claimed 'Cummings "only does angry and f***ing angry", said a minister. Johnson's language could be as bad. Critics in the party could be dismissed as "c***s" or even "utter c***s". So too was the editor of The Sunday Times. "Emma Tucker is a c***," he said, when he didn't like a story her paper had run.'

FARCE MAJEURE

Apr 22, 2023

Dear Mogg
Today's serialisation in the Times of what purports to be an account of my glorious reign at the helmet of the ship of state, claims I said 'I am the Führer. I am the King'. Outrageous slur. Of course, what I said was 'I am Caesar.'
Pox romana
Boris

Apr 22, 2023

Dear Raab
You are so right about this Kafka biz. You and me were just powerless cogs in the great machine of state harpooned by the woke, tofu-eating, anti-growth elite. And now we are flung to the dogs in the chill of the backbenches.
Hyperbolic hyperbolox
Boris

Apr 23, 2023

Dear Raab
Once, I hated you for being one of the backstabbers but now that you are like me, a wounded warrior, struck down by friendly fire, with our only allies the glorious Mail and Express, we are, like David and Goliath, comrades in arms.
Wisteria in nostril
Boris

MICHAEL ROSEN

Apr 23, 2023

Dear Mogg
The Mirror has dug up info on where we stayed over the Easter vac, as if it's iniquitous to stay at a relly's pad in the Caribbean. Yes, he's the guy tied up with that loan thing with the Chair of the Beeb but didn't Macbeth stay at Duncan's castle?
Honda ad
Boris

Apr 24, 2023

Dear Mogg
Now look who's come out of the woodworm? Simon Case! He's someone who owes everything to me, yet is now going to bite the hand that bleeds it. The greatest bout of ingratitude since the moment Lear sees how ungrateful Ophelia is.
Ant an dec
Boris

Apr 27, 2023

Dear Mogg
Glad to see my comments condemning antisemitism in the Labour Party appearing in the media. The great thing about me is there is no connection between what I condemn one day and what I might have said myself on another.
Scrotum panorama
Boris

FARCE MAJEURE

Apr 27, 2023

Dear Mogg
I have no idea why people are getting so het up that I want to give Dad a knighthood. He's a bloody fine chap. We know that he's done a fantastic job because the result of his work is me. I am like 'The Lion King': I am Mustafa son of Simba.
Hakuna cantata
Boris

Apr 28, 2023

Dear Mogg
Am much disconcerted to see the Beeb Chair, Robert Sharp going down over this loan fandango. If a chap can't steer another chap towards a pot of cash, then where are we? This is wokery gone mad.
Lucre in toga
Boris

Apr 28, 2023

Dear Mogg
I set a precedent - resign from public life and whinge afterwards. The Raab weasel did it, Kwarteng did it, and now Robert Sharp - or not-very-Sharp, as I call him. We are the victims here, being crucified by the wokerati.
Agnes dei
Boris

Apr 28, 2023

Dear Mogg
Would you bloody believe it! Wokerati, cultural marxists are calling for me to be investigated for my alleged role in the appointment of Roger Sharp as Chair of the BBC.

MICHAEL ROSEN

Was Churchill investigated for appointing Jonathan Dimbleby?
Chronologico bolocorama
Boris

Apr 29, 2023

Dear Mogg
Of course I chose Ronald Sharp to be Beeb boss. He's a nice guy, he did me a favour and he gave us a decent donation to keep Tory coffers full. He was as ideal for the job as Paris was the ideal husband for Juliet. Learn from the Bard, I say.
Cilla blac
Boris

Apr 29, 2023

Dear Mogg
Headline in Express: BBC Must Act to Silence Lineker. Good to see a serious paper taking a swipe at Gerry Lineker. Carol Voldemort and him are the new woke luvvie elite conspiracy that wrecked this country by getting me kicked out.
Chihuahua dogma
Boris

Apr 30, 2023

Dear Mogg
Outrageous headline in the wokeratis' gospel, the Guardian: at heart, it says, I am 'extraordinarily empty' - a quote about me from that Poundshop Plutarch, Anthony Neasden. And yet, I rise above these darts just as Cupid withstood Neptune's arrows.
Vivat trex
Boris

FARCE MAJEURE

May 1, 2023

Dear Mogg
Is there a way of slapping an injunction thingie on to this book about me by Andrew Seldon? I can just about put up with the inside lane Westminster jonnies reading it, but I'm cringing at the thought of it being available to all and sunday.
Harem scarem
Boris

Reply from John Wake:

Dear Boris
Once again, that Rosen has mistranscribed your remarkables. That should read, of course, "Ale and Sundae".
Your Pal Dave

May 1, 2023

Dear Mogg
I have of course been quoted as condemning the ghastly Guardian and their ghastly cartoon because I despise all racism and antisemitism. The wokerati will claim that I myself have said things that are a little racy but these were jests.
Hic hac ho ho ho
Boris

MICHAEL ROSEN

May 1, 2023

Dear Mogg
Can you remind me? Was the ghastly Cummings still in my employ when he went on about Goldman Sachs and their people with 'fingers in every pie' in the EU? I don't want that coming back to haunt me as the ghost of Hamlet's uncle haunts Hamlet.
Spectre al dente
Boris

May 1, 2023

Dear Mogg
Remind me, was it you or some other gent who quipped that Bercow and Letwin were illuminati? Just twixt thou and me, was this a covert jibe at you know who or just one of your random quips, like the ever-jovial Jacques in 'As You Like It'?
Ludo lido
Boris

May 3, 2023

Dear Mogg
I confess I'm perturbed that Anthony Smeldon's book about me is selling well. I should ask for a share in the royalties. I resent the fact that he is touring radio and TV studios on the back of doing a crotchet job on the great Boris.
Kleenex in nespresso
Boris

FARCE MAJEURE

May 3, 2023

Dear Mogg
I can feel in my heart that Friday will be a bad day for us with the local election results coming in like a wet rag to a bull. If only HQ had put me on the road I would have given the Party a storming victory just as Churchill did in 1945.
Duodenum pandemonium
Boris

May 5, 2023

Dear Mogg
A spot of bother brewing on the horizon with this clip of me in a car seemingly not wearing my life jacket. The Lib Dems are trying to stick up a kink about it as if I did it as some kind of deliberate Tory trick. It was just a judgment of error.
Ulcer in orbit
Boris

BBC data: The Conservatives lost control of more than 40 councils. Gains were shared by Labour, Liberal Democrats and Greens in all regions.

More than 1,000 Tory seats changed hands. Prime Minister Rishi Sunak says the loss of Conservative councillors is "disappointing".

MICHAEL ROSEN

May 5, 2023

Dear Mogg
These results show conclusively that I would have won this election. Labour would've been ground into the bust. How the backstabbers must be kicking themselves for having pushed me out as humiliatingly as Malvolio banishes Romeo.
Rectum spumante
Boris

May 6, 2023

Dear Mogg
And so the attention now returns to the key issue of the last 50 years: Partygate. I predict that the Kangaroo Court will fail in their effort to torpedo my fortress. Then, as the Sunak rocket crumbles, I will rise again like Phonics from the ashes.
Tepid aphid
Boris

May 6, 2023

Dear Mogg
How did the local election results go in my lovely constituency of Oxbridge and Riuslip? I fear that some of the old faithfuls were too skewy to sort out their i.d. as in 'Hamlet' when Polonium muddles his words. My return will herald a new lawn.
Hero in semolina
Boris

FARCE MAJEURE

No. 1597
5 May –
18 May 2023
£2.99

PRIVATE EYE

HISTORIC SOUVENIR ISSUE

MAN IN HAT SITS ON CHAIR

THIS ROYAL JOKE IS 100% RECYCLED

MICHAEL ROSEN

Television coverage showed Boris Johnson and his wife arriving with other former Prime Ministers at Westminster Abbey for the Coronation of Charles the third.

May 7, 2023

Dear Mogg
I confess that the old Corro didn't turn out to be quite as much of a Borisfest as I hoped it would be. Some nasty comments about my garb and engagingly tousled hair have sullied the occasion, just as Gecko's ghost spoils Macbeth's dinner party.
In vesta curri
Boris

May 7, 2023

Dear Mogg
How pathetic are they, the ministers being wheeled out on today's media shows! They think they know everything but the telephone in the room is me. They ignore me just as Aristotle ignored Hadrian's Wall.
Libera nose
Boris

During the Coronation service Penny Mordant, a Conservative MP and Leader of the House, was given sword carrying duties during the ceremony because of the ancient role she has as Lord President of the Council.

FARCE MAJEURE

MICHAEL ROSEN

May 7, 2023

Dear Mogg
It's all Mordant Mordant Mordant. I could have carried a sword as well as her. Or an axe. Or a skimitar. But no. I am demoted to the level of Gordon bloomin' Brown, an outcast on the fringes of fate like Churchill in his Blue Period.
Excalibur non sequitur
Boris

May 7, 2023

Dear Mogg
Seen this headline in Teleg? "Sunak blamed for 'knifing the most successful Tory election winner in 50 years'." Finally, the truth is out, just as Iago finds out how he was tricked by Othello.
Vivat Boris
Boris

May 8, 2023

Dear Mogg
The Mirror today has the slimy Gove saying that my reign as PM was 'chaotic' but 'entertaining' and that I would say things like 'what was it that Montezuma said?' Not so! I remember very well that Montezuma said, 'Alas, poor Yorick!'
Ad lib ultra geranium
Boris

FARCE MAJEURE

May 9, 2023

Dear Mogg
I'm all over the news for having 'squared up' to Charlie boy, over our Rwanda plan. Those were the days when this country had a PM with a bit of oomph, who could, as Lady Macduff says, stick it to the screwing stick.
Sub aqua gorgonzola
Boris

May 10, 2023

Dear Mogg
Wow, my bill to deal with the Kangaroo Court has reached 245k. Thank Jove (not Gove, hah!) that the taxpayer foots that little bill. Don't see why it should have to come out of my hard-won kitty.
Neutragena in martini
Boris

May 11, 2023

Dear Mogg
Trump and I share the same thing: we have been felled by backstabbers, naysayers, mountebanks and a sinister blob infected by wokeness. Just as AA Milne shows in 'The Lion, the Witch and the Bathrobe', we are heading for a Last Battle.
Faeces in Narnia
Boris

May 12, 2023

Dear Mogg
Are you following the kerfiffle about the school tests in the schools where poor children go? Did we have tests at Eton? TTTT, I've forgotten! I've always thought that we

need schools to be more like the boys battling it out in 'Lord of the Files'.
Belladonna summer
Boris

May 12, 2023

Dear Mogg
Did you see that claim in the Telegraph that I called Sue Gray a 'psycho'? Far-fetched! I remember that movie very well: one of Humphrey Bogarde's best performances so I'd hardly be calling Sue Grey that.
Risotto diva
Boris

May 15, 2023

Dear Mogg
How sweet to see the ever-restrained Priti Patel leaping to defend me in recent clashes with the backstabber sitting in my deserved seat as PM. I sense a groundswill amongst the party faithful seeking to restore me, just as Churchill was in 1960.
Dettol in texas
Boris

May 15, 2023

Dear Mogg
The Times says that my Day of Judgement with the Kangaroo Court is just 10 days away and that my loyal cohorts are cutting a deal which will see my wrist being slipped but I will avoid the chop as great heroes like Hamlet and me always do.
Cactus in cirrhosis
Boris

FARCE MAJEURE

May 15, 2023

Dear Mogg
Blah blah blah: the hacks are trying to deride my turbo-charged, oven-ready hospital building plan. One measly hospital gets a teensy bit behind in its building plans - probably due to navvies being lazy sods - and I get it in the nock.
Extra plasma in hydrangea
Boris

May 15, 2023

Dear Mogg
The Independent think they've got a scoop on me blocking the slimy Gove's knighthood. They say I had him down for a gong but pulled it as he blocked my glorious return last autumn, when, just as Jesus returned to Rome, I would be PM again.
Crypto penis in pesto
Boris

May 16, 2023

Dear Mogg
Wokery gone mad! I was pictured in the press looking fabulously fetching in a Firemen Sam outfit and now two of the tofu-eating, guardianista wokeists involved in the TV series are objecting. People like them are destroying Britain.
Sub sahara waleda
Boris

May 16, 2023

Dear Mogg
Hats off to the excellent Melanie Phipps writing in the

MICHAEL ROSEN

Times today decrying the BBC's use of the term 'Far Right' to describe us. The woke BBC should be calling us the So Right, as we've been so bang on about Brexit, Covid and the economy.
Extra balti
Boris

May 17, 2023

Dear Mogg
Standby for a mega-whinge from the anti-Boris mob because I've nominated 3 pals for peerages, incl the delectable Nadine. 'O woe woe,' they'll whine, 'Boris has lumbered us with 3 by-elections.' They're like Julius Caesar whingeing about Machiavelli.
Imodium panic
Boris

May 16, 2023

Dear Mogg
Traitor Gato Hurri is leaking all over the place. He claims I called Macron, 'Putin's lickspittle', and that I would 'punch his lights out'. Moi? I don't think so. I would have said it in French anyway: 'Macron, du bist ein Scheissgesicht.'
Lingua franca wanca
Boris

The National Conservatives held a three-day event in London starting 15th May entitled: NATCON UK. It was attended by several far-right conservative members of parliament, and political persons of the same persuasion from the USA including Kevin Roberts, President of the 'Heritage Foundation'.

FARCE MAJEURE

May 19, 2023

Dear Mogg
One of my great virtues is that I spot an opportunity and take it. What I believe is neither here nor there, though belief in the necessity that I be no 1 is constant. These lively Nat Cons seem like something I should be heading up.
Sciatica in avocado
Boris

May 19, 2023

Dear Mogg
I desperately fear that I am now in the ranks of the forgotten men, like Prithi Patel, Angela Leadsom and Theresa May, languishing forever in the desert of the backbenches. As Joseph Kurtz says to Conrad in 'The Trial': 'The horror! The horror!'
Aviva espana
Boris

May 19, 2023

Dear Mogg
The Teleg says I stand no chance of standing in my old beloved constituency of Hanley-on-Thames. HQ is going to block it. We shall see. My powers of persuasion are as great as when the ghost of Hamlet convinces his father to murder Mercutio.
Avanti panti
Boris

MICHAEL ROSEN

May 19, 2023

Dear Mogg
The ranks of wokery have taken to scanning the backbenches to see if we're turning up or not as if we're nothing more than day labourers. It is privilege enough for the people of Oxbridge and Risulip to be represented by a figure of my statue.
Verruca in fusilli
Boris

May 22, 2023

Dear Mogg
I think things are getting a trifle hot for poor Suella. I suspect she's being sandbagged by tofu-eating cultural wokists. You'll remember Romeo couldn't stand Cleopatra. Same thing.
Prima donna salmonella
Boris

May 22, 2023

Dear Mogg
Tragically, my major oeuf on Shakespeare is delayed. Have been toying with a title: Boris Caesar, Et Tu Boris, A Bard in the Hand is Worth Two in the Bush...but nothing feels right yet. Have told publishers, can't write it, till I've got a title.
Contra contracto
Boris

FARCE MAJEURE

May 22, 2023

Dear Mogg
Good government is all about what you can wangle and finagle. Lovely Suella is an expert wangler and finagler. She did what she could to get out of being done for speeding. Hamlet didn't want to take the rap for murdering Malvolio.
Sod erat demonstrandum
Boris

May 22, 2023

Dear Mogg
Oh now the meaty have fallen! I see that Sunak is being accused of using my 'playbook' by delaying coming to a decision on whether lovely Suella is in trouble over the driving infringery. I can say, hand on hearth, I am a trialblazer.
Homeric rumbaba
Boris

May 23, 2023

Dear Mogg
With Raab slipping out the back door, with Savid Jajid, the silly boy Hancock and gorgeous Nadine all with flights booked to board rooms and mediafests in arcadia, do we wonder if the timetick is bombing away under lovely Suella?
Detritus in parti
Boris

MICHAEL ROSEN

May 23, 2023

Dear Mogg
Every lining has a silver cloud. You know what all these dismissals and resignations mean, don't you? A Siege Garrulous sits empty and ready for me at the Westminster Round Table. I am Sir Gahalad in waiting.
Ultra tampon in delphinium
Boris

May 23, 2023

Dear Mogg
The obnoxious Reyner woman has asked in the House if Suella told her special adviser to tell journalists that there was no speeding ticket, when there was. This is the kind of nasty sniping from woke trots like Raynar that brought ME down.
Quiz in guano
Boris

May 23, 2023

Dear Mogg
I try very hard not to gloat at Sunak's discomfiture over Suella's misdemeanours but as Oprah Winston says, 'What's round goes round'. Btw could you do a quick inventory on how many kids I've got and what their names are?
Fortnum et raisin
Boris

FARCE MAJEURE

May 23, 2023

Dear Mogg
Have you seen the Independent (woke trotskyite rag)? They've snitched that I did a bloody good impression of little Macron (Micron, actually) with his French accent. It's important for Brits to mock foreigners' accents. It shows we're best.
Simulatio in tiramisu
Boris

May 24, 2023

Dear Mogg
I'm circling the waggons. Wherever I look, whatever I do, they pull another cat out of the bag. This is Pandora boxing, I tell you. They will stop at nothing to have me in stitches. But I'm fighting back, just as Mercutio defeated Macbeth.
Mascarpone tremens
Boris

May 24, 2023

Dear Mogg
We have to present a united font over Partygate. Politically motivated weasels are careering my sabotage. We must deny them access to my WhatsUpp messages.
Minibus in reverso
Boris

May 25, 2023

Dear Mogg
Never in the history of mankind can Macduff's words have been so opposite: 'sound and fury dignifying

MICHAEL ROSEN

nothing' - thus do the fleas seeking to sting me, drag me down to the heights of Babylon. 'Revenge!' the ghost of Omelette's father cries.
Multiplex inertia
Boris

May 25, 2023

Dear Mogg
I see that the front bench is backsliding on my great pledge to build 400 hospitals. They're now talking about putting it off till 2030. Just as Hamlet delays killing Caliban in the famous 'Now might I do it, Pat' speech, so do they.
Toxic domino
Boris

May 25, 2023

Dear John Royle
You appear to have addressed your query to Michael Rosen. He knows nothing. I am the great writer of this missive. I doubt whether you've spotted a misstake, as I am fautless.
Campari olivetti
Boris

John Royle replied:

Dear Boris Posen
You are indeed faultless and I shall admonish myself most severely for my outlandish temerity in questioning your wording.
Torta umile
John

FARCE MAJEURE

May 25, 2023

Dear Don Joyle
Thanks for your note. I hope that once I've become Lord Boris of Cotswoldia you will come and visit me.
Hades in rus
Boris

Margaret Ferrier was an MP for the SNP party for the Rutherglen and Hamilton West constituency. It came to light that she had broken rules during the pandemic in September 2020 by testing positive for Covid and still travelling on a train from Glasgow to London. She was suspended from the SNP but still attended parliament in London as an independent member. On the 6th June MP's voted for her to be suspended. At this point in time this had not progressed any further.

May 25, 2023

Dear Mogg
Worrying situation re Ferrier the Scots Nat due for suspension. If she goes down for 30 days so could I and that would be party over for Boris. It's a time bomb, like the one that killed Julius Caesar.
Campari yoda
Boris

May 26, 2023

Dear Mogg
The Independent says I'm 'furious' and 'in despair' over the fact that cops are grubbing through the records of our jolly times at Checquers during Lockdowns. They are like Rosenstern and Guildencrantz spying on Hamlet's father.
Unisex matador
Boris

MICHAEL ROSEN

May 26, 2023

Dear Mogg
How dare they try to take my honours list away from me! It's an insult to the fact that I once held the highest office in the land rover. When Mark Antony stood before the mob and honoured Socrates, did Polonius deny him?
Nadine nadir
Boris

May 26, 2023

Dear Mogg
At least Gato Hurri sticks up for me. He is all over the media today presenting a measured view in tones that remind me of this great young Welsh singer, Louis Capaldi who's making a wave at the moment.
Pontipool pilate
Boris

May 26, 2023

Dear Mogg
I'm in the US at the moment. I've pigeon-holed Trump and told him that if he gets in, he'd bloomin' better back me on Ukraine. I felt like Churchill when he nagged LBJ to repel Russia from Vietnam.
Diplomatico duplo
Boris

"UK ministers engaged in bitter fight to halt release of Covid secrets"

The Observer - May 27, 2023

FARCE MAJEURE

Covid inquiry is sticking to its 48-hour deadline to hand over unredacted messages and notes between Johnson and his ministers during the pandemic. The government this weekend is standing firm in its refusal to divulge the material.

May 27, 2023

Dear Mogg
My former deputy chief of staff, Chloe Watson, is touring TV studios, draping her gazelle legs over the couch, dragging my dirt through the name. She reminds me of Othello badmouthing Prospero. As the Beatles sang, 'Get off of my cloud!'
Ronaldo cantona
Boris

May 29, 2023

Dear Mogg
The Barclay boy is backsliding over my 400 new hospitals plan. He's admitting they're not actually all whole new hospitals. This is the Party without me at its helmet: full of wimps who can no more sell a pup than Juliet's father can in Othello.
Festes testes
Boris

May 29, 2023

Dear Mogg
It feels so good to be back in the headlines again even if I have been dried out to hang. I will deal with the treachery of underlings just as Falstaff sees off Hal in Twelfth Night.
Tinnitus in ascot
Boris

CL

MICHAEL ROSEN

Shaun Wing wrote:

Dear Boris
My MoggMail is full of praise for their favourite white-blond barbarian. They sing from the chimney tops like fiddler on the roof: "some will never rest until the roly-poly rolls out of town." Hounded by the hound dogs, "clamantis" all the time.
Raucous Brutus
Smugg

"Phillip Schofield 'hung out to dry' as recriminations fester over This Morning exit"

Daily Telegraph - May 21, 2023

Presenter said to feel heartbroken and betrayed by Holly Willoughby, but his detractors say he has got his comeuppance.

May 29, 2023

Dear Mogg
Will this Philip Skyfall story carry on keeping my Covid diaries out of the headlines? As it happens he was very helpful to me right at the moment I was weighing up whether to go for herd immunity. No one cares about that stuff though.
Amnesia blotto
Boris

FARCE MAJEURE

May 31, 2023

Dear Mogg
This Lady Hazlitt is clearly an undercover woke Trotskyite socialite. Or socialist. Soon methinks we'll need our friends to rubbish her as a lefty lawyer, danger to the people. Obviously true: she didn't go to a good school. Just a Grammar.
Plebs in hydrangea
Boris.

May 31, 2023

Dear Mogg
Revealing my messages would be a breach of National Security. That's because the British people knew that National Security was safe in my hands - as safe as the ship that brings Ferdinand to the island in 'The Tempest of the Shrew'.
Pro mega beano
Boris

May 31, 2023

Dear Mogg
I was papped at the village fete near the much beloved constituency of Hanley-on-Thames which has stoked rumours that I might be throwing my ring into the hat there for selection as their candidate. As if!
Cynical bingo
Boris

MICHAEL ROSEN

May 31, 2023

Dear Mogg
There's an excellent article up on the internet about why my smile has helped win elections. It shows how I dash a cutting figure and people respond to me with affection and adulation and it's why Persil loved to look into Medusa's eyes.
Comatose in Skopelos
Boris

May 31, 2023

Dear Mogg
People take pleasure in rubbishing the deal I struck with the EU prior to the conspiracy that felled me. 'Chaos!' they whimper. I had every sympathy with the EU, much inspired, when young, by Email and the Detectives by Eric Clapton.
Ex libris elba
Boris

In preparation for the Covid Inquiry, the leader of the Inquiry, Baroness Hallett has asked the government to provide documents and transcripts of phone and mobile messages such as those on the Whatsapp messaging system.

FARCE MAJEURE

May 31, 2023

Dear Mogg
Just settling into a nice slew of white wine spitzers while trying to follow what Sunak et al are saying about my WhatsUpp messages. Are they irrelevant or irreverent? Luckily, I can write thish because sure as holly I can't say it!
Leen tu in gardino
Boris

May 31, 2023

Dear Mogg
You see how cunning I am, just like Baldric in Black Mirror? By sending in all my WhatsUpp messages etc. I make it really diff. for Sunak et al to withhold theirs. And that, Moggo, is how to blame the spread.
Post meridian onion
Boris

Jun 1, 2023

Dear Mogg
When Samsung brought the temple down on Delilah's head, little did he know then that when Boris came to do the same with Number 10, the people would rise up and acclaim him as the true leader just as they chose Churchill in 1945.
Hosanna in victoria station
Boris

MICHAEL ROSEN

Jun 1, 2023

Dear Mogg
Revenge on the backstabber! Sunak is caught between two stiles: if he refuses to reveal, Lady Hazlitt will have his garters for guts; if he releases them, he'll reveal more than Lady Jane Grey parading through the streets of Coventry.
Mars rolo marco polo
Boris

Jun 1, 2023

Dear Mogg
I'm sitting in the sun quaffing a turbo-charged snifter so excuse any faultlines in this missive. 30 mins to go. The deadloom lines for backstabber Sunak. As Conrad Joseph says: 'The merry trade of death and dance' but I live on.
Tempus fuxit
Boris

Jun 1, 2023

Dear Mogg
Sunak's bottled it. He knows there's stuff in there that'll drag him down with me. Lady Hazlitt will have to order his arrest. What japes to see Plod knocking on the door of Numero 10, eh? As Bob Monkhouse sang, 'I shot the sheriff...'
Vivat reggae
Boris

FARCE MAJEURE

Jun 2, 2023

Dear Mogg
People are falling hook, line and stinker for my 'offer' to the Inquiry that they can have my WhatsUpp messages! The whole point is that these only go back to April 2021. The really juicy stuff that might incriminate me was earlier!
Bruschetta in error
Boris

Jun 2, 2021

Dear Mogg
Are you going into the House much? I find it unutterably tedious. What is the point of being a backbencher? I am a leader of men. Destiny shapes my destiny. As Caesar said, 'Beware the ideas of March'.
Sub aquarius
Boris

Jun 2, 2023

Dear Mogg
Odious Gatto Hurri is spilling the bees, claiming I said I was 'bored' of the whole testing shambles and that I yelled at Jajid Savid. I am a great sculptor of words so, yes, at times I am indiscreet, but that's why I'm charming and successful.
Caffe hero
Boris

MICHAEL ROSEN

Jun 3, 2023

Dear Mogg
This latest brouhahahaha has scuppered work on my memoir. I had just reached the point at which I saved Britain through inventing the Covid vaccine just as Verona saves Scotland in Macbeth.
Salvator vibrator
Boris

Jun 3, 2023

Dear Mogg
The paps are undermining my dignity by catching me at unfortunate moments of disarray as regards my nether regions. If a great statesman like me can't be given leeway with his trousers, where are we as a nation?
Crevice Britannia
Boris

Jun 3, 2023

Dear Mogg
I picked up a thing or two from a guy in the Magic Circle: at the very moment you 'reveal', you 'conceal'. The whole world thinks I've 'handed over' the whole truth, while in fact, they've got nothing from me for the time the Corunnavirus hit us.
Occludo ludo
Boris

FARCE MAJEURE

CLVIII

MICHAEL ROSEN

Jun 3, 2023

Dear Mogg
I gather that Manchester United have won the Soccer Cup. That's good. That club are a fine example of entrepreneurial spirit that has made Britain great and only British players have the pluck to beat the foreign team they were up against.
Rectum in cranium
Boris

Jun 3, 2023

Dear Mogg
More heat than light being brewed in Covidgate so I have retreated to a cool room in Cotswoldia, with a good supply of Pimms while Antonio Capaldi's beautiful Four Seasons symphony plays on the gramophone.
Tranquil espadrille
Boris

Jun 4, 2023

Dear Mogg
The appalling woke-sheet, the Guardian, headlines with questions that could 'sink' Sunak and me. Piffle! I am unsinkable.
Titanic ego
Boris

FARCE MAJEURE

Jun 4, 2023

Dear Mogg
Terrific front page in Mail on Sunday: Labour declares class war on Middle Britain. Exactly. Get off our patch, Labour. Class war is our thing, but we do it responsibly: keeping wages down and cutting public spending, which is good for Britain.
Penuri in toto
Boris

Michael Rosen tweeted:

News in: an exciting advance has been made in how society can cure its ills and make major advances, even faster and greater than AI. It's called Fuk-U. The basic principle behind Fuk-U is that it's directed at anyone being non-productive. This way, we become more productive.

Jun 4, 2023

Dear Mogg
It's hotting up, Moggo. Some of the hacks are on to it. They're saying that the WhatsUPP messages may reveal the backstabbers' plot to oust me. The plot thickens just as Macbeth thickened the plot to oust Horatio.
Schema con fungi
Boris

Jun 5, 2023

Dear Mogg
Yawn, yawn. Parliament back from recess. I really can't be fagged to sit on those bloomin' back benches like I'm a walk-on in a World War 2 film like 'Forrest Dump'. As

the Bard says, 'Fear no more the heat of the oven'.
Ikea tedium
Boris

Jun 6, 2023

Dear Mogg
They're persecuting me: I might not get public funding for all this legal flim-flam. As Othello says in 'King Lear', "As gods to wanton boys are we to the flies". It matters not, earthlings! I can raise the dosh through the back passage.
Colonic lucre
Boris

Jun 7, 2023

Dear Mogg
The polls are looking great for me in my beloved constituency of Oxbridge and Riuslip. The naysayers, backstabbers and the woke rabble have been crying woe bestride thee Boris, just as Cassandra predicted disaster in Macbeth.
Anal rictus
Boris

Jun 7, 2023

Dear Mogg
The hacks are whingeing that I won't do interviews in Cotswoldia. I'm on a powerful fitness regime to face the rigours of heavy lunching during my world lecture tours. I hold the conch, as they say in William Godalming's 'Lord of the Files'.
Mucus in Londis
Boris

FARCE MAJEURE

Jun 7, 2023

Dear Mogg
Too bloody right: the Cabinet Office has defended my right to have my £245 thou Partygate legal bill paid. I'm a former PM, for god's sake, not some street sleeper sponging off the state, stealing tax-payers' money. I'm not Roddy Biggs, am I?
Felonius monk
Boris

Shaun Wing posted:

Dear Boris
Goodness, my MoggoMailbox is a rustling mattress of grubby notes from the deprived existing on powdered cuppaSoups&dandelionSeeds - informing Yours Truly to send it on to Boris for his "legalis quadrigis." My Son Sepsis is setting up a Just Shafting page.
Smugg

Jun 8, 2023

Dear Mogg
At last some good news: traitor Sunak has finally accepted my excellent Honours List, which will elevate people who've served the greatest prime minister of recent times, just as Iago serves Othello: with loyalty, integrity and truth.
Taurus faeces motto
Boris

Jun 8, 2023

Dear Mogg
Gato Hurri has leaked the story that I briefed you to give Sunak hell. They say I gave you carte blanche to be a

pain in his backside and I suppose this is to prove that I am as disloyal as some kind of woke Trot. Am I perfidion Albious?
Rectal inferno
Boris

Jun 8, 2023

Dear Mogg
The Kangarooo Court have handed me some kind of 'dossier' (a German word) which they say contains their allegations against me. Everywhere I look, the woke establishment is firing its guns at me, but I am as steady as an ocean liner.
Bella Lusitania
Boris

Donald Trump has been charged by the judiciary of the United States with the illegal retention of documents containing secret information relating to the military of the United States and its diplomatic relationships with other countries. The indictment includes the removal of documents to his home in Florida that should have been kept within the security system of the White House. He has also been charged with obstructing the FBI who went to his home in Mar-a-Largo to retrieve these documents.

Jun 9, 2023

Dear Don
I see the Woke Mob are saying you tried to conceal stuff after they issued you with subpoenis for their return. So, with the Kangaroo Court! All part of the liberal elite conspiracy. It's Spartacus locking up Aristotle all over again.
Sphincter botox
Boris

FARCE MAJEURE

Jun 9, 2023

Dear Mogg
I have a new ally. Incredibly, the London Mayor Sajid Khan has praised the fact that it was me who introduced the Combustion Zone in London, not some Woke Green like that MP, Christine Lucas who now says she's throwing in the towel rail.
Negroni detox
Boris

Jun 9, 2023

Dear Nadine
Sometimes the best of laid plans of men and mice are thwarted by mean-minded traitors. They will live to regret this, just as Othello regretted he had killed Juliet. Remember Edith Proof's song, 'je ne regrette ron'.
Tragedia multimedia
Boris

Jun 9, 2023

Dear Nadine
O my heart is heavy, my soul weeps to see thee depart. As Bob Monkhouse sang so memorably, 'No woman, no cry'. Your place on the benches will be forever yours, with Nadine Doris, inscribed in my mind. Hamlet said it all: 'I am dying Egypt, dying.'
Paean oconcerto
Boris

To everyone's surprise, on this day, Boris Johnson stepped down from his position as the Member of Parliament for Uxbridge and Ruislip. The BBC news page reported that "Mr. Johnson said he had decided to step down 'for now' after an investigation into the Partygate scandal carried out by the Privileges Committee."

Jun 9, 2023

Dear Mogg
You must be wondering why, in the light of the momentous events of today, I haven't penned you a note. Indeed. This is one of the most extraordinary events in British, if not world, history. But remember, it's not over till the fat lady swings.
Exit oscar
Boris

Jun 10, 2023

Dear Mogg
As the sun rises in the West over Cotswoldia, I'm minded of 'King Lear': "There's a divinity that shapes our ends". Yes, my end is shaped. I am inspired by Churchill's returns from the cold, like Captain Oates the Arctic explorer.
Lyceum panto
Boris

Jun 10, 2023

Dear Mogg
At least I was able to wangle you a knighthood before I bid farewell to the great stage that I've presented with my grace. I quote the Bard and say to myself, 'Stand not upon the going of your order, Boris.' We greats live to fight again, Sir Jacob.
Quit squit
Boris

FARCE MAJEURE

> **PeterHardwiick17 wrote:**
>
> To Michael Rosen
> Rumour has it he resigned purely to screw up your chance of doing volume two of his letters.

Jun 10, 2023

Dear Mogg
It's Remainers' Revenge - an unholy alliance between the traitors within our ranks and the north London Metropolitan elite lefty lawyer cancel culture opposed to us. Acropolis said it all: 'The croaking frog doth bellow for revenge.'
Omerta in bognor regis
Boris

"BORIS: I've been forced out by a witch-hunt"

Daily Mail - Jun 10, 2023

The Ex Prime Minister quits as an MP because of the criticism of the 'Kangaroo Court' investigation into Partygate.

Jun 10, 2023

Dear Mogg
The offers are rolling in. My lips are sealed but you can choose which you think are the most likely: Spectator, Mail, Telegraph, GBNews, TimesRadio, Express, Sun, LBC, Newsnight, HIGNFY, QT, Vogue, CBeebies, CNN, AlJazeera or all of them!
In media des res
Boris

MICHAEL ROSEN

Nigel Adams is the MP for Selby and Ainsty. He was appointed a Minister without Portfolio by Boris Johnson in September 2021. He resigned as from the 12th June 2023.

Jun 10, 2023

Dear Nigel Adams
I don't know you but I salute you. There is no higher mission in life than to stand by one's leader. Your resignation will prove to be hugely discomforting for Sunak, which is marvellous. I am fiercely loyal to me too.
Gloria me gloria gaynor
Boris

Jun 10, 2023

Dear Mogg
My plan: I have a platform with a major news outlet; continue my lucrative lecture tours; pose next to a tank in Ukraine; safe seat selects me as their candidate; Sunak or successor resigns; I stand; am elected; I return! In triumph per Persepolice
Boris

Jun 10, 2023

Dear Boris
I'm a man of high moral principles. However, it is also my view that you, Boris, should never be constrained by such concerns as you were destined for higher things. The honour you've bestowed on me has helped me clarify my mind on this matter.
Simper fidelis
Sir Jacob

FARCE MAJEURE

Jun 12, 2023

Dear Mogg
Do you know that the Appointments Committee (aka the Disappointments Committee) rejected 8 of my nominations for peerages? We are living in a vicious totalitarian state, Moggo, in which a man can no longer take liberties.
Liza minelli in conga
Boris

Jun 12, 2023

Dear Mogg
When Tammy Wynette sang 'Stand by Me', he wouldn't have known that that number would be the theme song for my comeback. You've stood by me, Moggo. The French word for 'strong' is 'fort' and their word for 'rock' is 'roque'. You are my roquefort.
Costa cutta
Boris

Jun 12, 2023

Dear Mogg
Exciting development: Farage has been on to me with the idea to set up an alliance to 'defend the Brexit legacy'. Legacy? Is there a legacy? Could you send me a briefing on it so I can sound like I'm somewhere in the right balls park?
Farrago panacea
Boris

MICHAEL ROSEN

Jun 12, 2023

Dear Mogg
I may divide opinion as regards my genius, but I note that though John Major used to be dismissed by some, he is now highly respected. In time, I too will be universally loved as much as Voldemort from the J.K.Potter series.
Hernia ex libris
Boris

Jun 12, 2023

Dear Mogg
Now as the cold day of light lifts, we can see who are our allies, and who are the vicious, snide, cowardly, backstabbing, deserting, mutineers. Remember Paul Simon and Art Cumberbatch's song 'Old Friends' - and look what happened to them.
Vast deferens
Boris

Jun 12, 2023

Dear Mogg
People I thought I could trust are now nothing more than a regiment of Deserting Rats. Yes, they may have defeated Beau Brummell at the Battle of El Allgemeine, but they didn't turn on their own leader, the great Monty Don.
Pro patria moriarti
Boris

FARCE MAJEURE

Jun 12, 2023

Dear Mogg
If you see anything in any of my missives to you which suggest that I'm losing my hold on reality, you will tell me won't you, and I will know when my time is up. Even Macbeth spoke of the last syllabub of recorded time.
Linoleum stamina
Boris

Jun 12, 2023

Dear Mogg
Just as Shakespeare left behind his abrasive memoirs that reveal so much of his life and times, so I will talk of how I shaped an epoch in the memoir I am writing. All who stood in my way, will be scythed down with my oven-charged turbos.
Ozymandias randias
Boris

Jun 12, 2023

Dear Mogg
My outrage at the vetting committee vetoing 8 of my choices is mitigated by their approval of Charlotte's peerage. This neatly bucks the pass to them - the hacks will be chasing them for the next year trying to find out why they OK'd it!
Turdus transfer
Boris

"NADINE DORRIES: The sinister forces that stopped me, a girl born into poverty in Liverpool, from reaching the House of Lords"

Daily Mail - Jun 13, 2023

MICHAEL ROSEN

Jun 12, 2023

Dear Mogg
Nadine has written in the Mail about how 'sinister forces' are thwarting my efforts to put her in the Lords. Indeed. Indeed: they are like the Witches in 'Twelfth Night'. Beware the Ideas of March, Moggo.
Malefactor in tractor
Boris

David Lee@t_david_Lee wrote:

Dear de Piffle
May I gently remind you that the appropriate form of address now is no longer "Dear Mogg" but "Dear Sir Jacob". Etonium debretts eleison Sir Jacob, G.B. Nws. (and bar)

Jun 14, 2023

Dear Mogg
News is out that I demanded that Sunak let me give Dad a peerage. What's wrong with that? Dad is a great guy, really funny, great opinions, he loves me, I love him, everyone loves him. It's just as everyone loves Norman Bates in 'Spider-man'.
Psycho gecko
Boris

Sir Bernard Jenkin is a member of the Conservative party serving on the cross-party Privileges Committee. He has been an MP for Harwich and North Essex since 2010.

FARCE MAJEURE

Jun 14, 2023

Dear Mogg
Have you seen my coup de grease? I've demanded that Bernard Jenkins resign. That'll set the chickens amongst the cats. He'll no more be able to wriggle out of that one than King Lear could escape blame for the death of Hotspur.
Sordid circus
Boris

Jun 14, 2023

Dear Nadine
You have thrown a spammer in the works! No one knows when you're going to resign, the whole world is on tenterhoops. Now the backstabbers will regret their treachery just as Sumatra sang, 'Regrets I've had a few...'
Patio teriyaki
Boris

Jun 15, 2023

Dear Mogg
See how the locusts and vultures descend on me like torpedoes holing an oak tree. This report is a tustle of lies designed to besmirch the topless towers of aluminium. In the meantime: I'm seeking solstice in liquid sustenance.
Alcopop ad turbo turbo
Boris

MICHAEL ROSEN

Jun 15, 2023

Dear Mogg
I return and repel their jibes and scourges with carefully chosen bon-nose of my own. When the General Election sinks Sunak beneath the clouds, the people will summon me as their avenging angel.
Bovril gladiator
Boris

Jun 15, 2023

Dear Mogg
As Churchill said, 'Now this is not the end. It is not even ending the beginning. But it is, perhaps, beginning to end the ending at the beginning.' Mystic Meg's deranged knife-thrust will be parried by the sherried ranks of my loyal cohorts.
Branston pendulum
Boris

Jun 15, 2023

Dear Mogg
See how magnanimous I am, urging our colleagues not to vote against the Kangaroo court's report! Like Uriah Heap in 'Great Expectations', I am forgiving, honest and humble. As Vivien Leigh played by Scarlett O'Hara says, 'Tomorrow is another day'.
Ad lib debris
Boris

FARCE MAJEURE

Jun 15, 2023

Dear Mogg
I think we need to raise the argument onto a new level: we should move off saying, 'You can't know whether I was lying', and saying instead 'What's wrong with lying? Lying is good government.' It's time to get honest about lying.
Max factor in chorus
Boris

Jun 16, 2023

Dear Mogg
The great Mel Brooks play 'The Crucible' shows us how a witch hunt can destroy the lives of innocent people. It anticipates my plight in the face of a ruthless kangaroo. But we have a guiding light: Nadine. She is our Joan of Ark.
Ave Maria
Dorris

Jun 16, 2023

Dear Mogg
Hard at work writing my new column for a certain great national daily paper whose name begins with 'M' and rhymes with 'tail'. Secrets stay safe with me. These articles will help me eke out a living and show the world I was right about everything.
Gaudeamus
Boris

MICHAEL ROSEN

Jun 16, 2023

Dear Mogg
I have various other projects up my back burner like a series of children's books about a lovable old teddy who keeps getting into trouble over silly little things like having a teddy bear's picnic when he's not supposed to.
Ad fib comedian
Boris

Jun 16, 2023

Dear Mogg
Though this Mail job gives me the perfect platform to reclaim my rightful place at the heart of the British people's heart, I fear it may drag me away from my 2 great projects: a) my great hors d'oeuvre on Shakespeare and c) my memoirs.
Persona non grater
Boris

Jun 16, 2023

Dear Mogg
In some ways, the UK is too small a stage for me. I'm minded of the Status Quota hit, 'Rockin' All Over the World'. Perhaps NATO, the UN, the G7 (or all four), looking for someone with diplomatic no-how, will turn to me to be their special envy.
Mappa mondeo
Boris

FARCE MAJEURE

Jun 16, 2023

Dear Mogg
Was Napoleon defeated? No. He overcame the woke blob. I learn from le petit chaparral that we are not only fighting our foes but we combat the washy-wishy, milk-shop cowards who, as Simon Garfunkel sings, 'pour oil on the bridge over troubled waters'.
Bluster plus
Boris

Jun 17, 2023

Dear Mogg
I may run out of ideas for this earth-breaking column I'm writing for the Mail (a million smackeroonies, eh? Not so bad.) If you think of anything that might stick a few boxes, can you send it my way? Man of the people stuff, s'il vous plate.
Vox plopuli
Boris

Jun 17, 2023

Dear Mogg
I am imagining the world sitting down to breakfast pouring over my jeu d'aspro in today's Mail. O how they were expecting a plangent diatribe about Sunak but - hah! - They got jokes about slimming just as Romeo mocks Falstaff. I am so good.
Gargantua in mantua
Boris

MICHAEL ROSEN

Michael Rosen tweeted:

I've been trying for 3 years to create the idea that Johnson screws up his quotes and then in his very first article for the Daily Mail, he claims that Julius Caesar 'said' something when it was really Shakespeare making it up, not the historical Julius Caesar!

Jun 17, 2023

Dear Mogg
Slight editing probby with my article in today's Mail. I said it was Julius Caesar himself who spaffed on about 'lean and hungry' Cassius and left out that it was of course the Bard's words. Funny thing that - detail has always been my strong point.
Omit vomit
Boris

Jun 17, 2023

Dear Mogg
Everyone loves dogs, don't they? For next week's column, why don't I write about our dog? I can show the world how, in spite of the brickbants that have been hurled at me, deep down, I'm Mr Nice. I love my dog.
Canis in tombola
Boris

FARCE MAJEURE

Jun 17, 2023

Dear Mogg
The great pillars of state are crumbling in the hands of counterfeiting traitors and Calvinistic killjoys. Why should the upper peletons of society fit their mean-minded template? As Falstaff says, 'we are alone and palely loitering.'
Ubi dubi du
Boris

Jun 18, 2023

Dear Mogg
Have to admit we're in a wee cul de sock: we've spent our whole lives telling people to respect the instruments of government and now we're telling them that these instruments are stuffed full of corrupt woke elite traitors.
Contradicta in Cotswoldia
Boris

Jun 18, 2023

Dear Rishi
I know we're not the best of amigos but I'm going to suggest that we bury the mallet and you cancel the general election. Dangerous forces are swirling about in the labyrinth beneath the whirlpool. Wake up Britain!
Fasces contra faeces
Boris

Jun 18, 2023

Dear Mogg
I've just seen that Lockdown video of you saying 'This party is not going to be investigated by the police' and 'we're all socially distanced'. Nice irony, Moggo but I'm

marginally concerned it IS going to be investigated by the police, tho.
Moralio vacuum
Boris

Jun 18, 2023

Dear Mogg
Remind me, did that ECRH thing find that Corbyn (or was it the Labour party?) did something illegal? Or was it unlawful? Either way, we roasted him (ha ha) but I'm a tad worried that our zeal to get him will come back to bite us.
Gluteus maximus masticatus
Boris

Jun 18, 2023

Dear Mogg
You and I are deeply religious folk. We know that one day we will meet our Maker. This brings order and purpose to our lives in ways that unbelievers can't comprehend even if there is always one 'Last Salsa in Paris'.
Mitsubishi in toto
Boris

Jun 19, 2023

Dear Mogg
I'm watching you in the Commons right now. You're in scintillating form. The woke Trotskyist mob opposite will never recover. Your analogy with Communist China is spot on. Everyone can see that Chairman Harman is Chairman Mao.
Polyfilla in acropolis
Boris

FARCE MAJEURE

The findings of the Privileges Committee were put to the House of Commons. The Committee's report had found that Mr Johnson deliberately misled the House and the Committee with regard to parties at Number 10 Downing Street during the period of Covid-19 lockdown regulations. In so doing he had "committed a serious contempt". Members of Parliament were asked to vote on the acceptability of the Committee's report. After five hours of debate, MPs voted by 354 to seven to approve the report. Approximately 200 conservative MPs did not vote. Rishi Sunak, the Prime Minister did not attend the debate and so did not vote.

Jun 19, 2023

Dear Mogg
I'll be watching the vote today from the heart of Cotswoldia counting the traitors and lily-livered abstainers. Remember the proverb: a company is known by the man it keeps. No matter! I'll put this squalid matter of fame and fortune behind me.
Narcissus in costco
Boris

Jun 19, 2023

Dear Mogg
In spite of your valiant efforts, a mere 7 loyal troopers have stood by me, their great leader. The song says it: 'Seven, seven the lily-white boys.' Remember Desdemona: 'When they shall die, take them and cut them out in little stars.'
O hubris verdegris
Boris

MICHAEL ROSEN

FARCE MAJEURE

Jun 19, 2023

Dear Rishi
I know we're dawn daggers, but I would like to say I respect your high principle of not being in the House for the vote tonight. Your excellent weaselling reminds me of me! Look what Hamlet achieved by ducking out of the fight with Romeo!
Canberra in canelloni
Boris

Jun 20, 2023

Dear Mogg
Regroup! You and I must bunker down in our hunkers and look to where the next fissures appear in the Woke elite's balustrade. As Jesus said, 'Fissures of men!' That Victoria Hertfordshire on Newsnight worries me. What's undone cannot be done.
Syntax random torpedo
Boris

Jun 20, 2023

Dear Mogg
I'm quoted in the Times today: 'there's always another innings'. Yes! As the sun sets in the east behind the pavilion, I wonder if the great Captain in the sky will call me up for one more Test Match. Did Plato not give Caesar one more chance?
Galactic geranium
Boris

The Newsreader, Clive Myrie presented 'Have I Got News for You'. He made several jokes about Boris Johnson as did the members of the panel. Clive Myrie was due to read news shortly after the programme but was replaced by another BBC staff member. It was simply a scheduling matter.

___
Jun 20, 2023

Dear Mogg
Am at a bit of a loser end at the moment. Given that that Clive Marie chap is out of the picture, I wondered if I should drop the Beeb a line and ask if I can do the News instead. I'd be superb: like Mark Antony when he pays tribute to Mercutio.
Orator in bisto
Boris

___
Jun 23, 2023

Dear Nadine
You've gott'em guessing! You say you're resigning but you don't! Genius. You are the mysterious smile that plays across the lips of the Mona Liza. The Enigma Variation of Elgar's 'Sphinx'. (This heat has me a tad piggledy-higgledy. You too?)
Amor vincit omnibus
Boris

___
Jun 23, 2023

Dear Mogg
Have written a superb column in the Mail today. I talk of Hubris and Nemesis, the two characters in Plato's great play 'Oedipus Trex'. And I make a special effort to give Ash Shergar a kicking. Next week? Hyperbole and Thermos, I think.
Scribo in lavatorium
Boris

FARCE MAJEURE

Jun 23, 2023

Dear Baelish
Please don't address your missives to that charlatan and ignoranus, Rosen. I am the epistola gigantibus round here.
Scylla and Chrysallis
Boris

Jun 24, 2023

Dear Mogg
Seen the profile of the slimy Gove in the Times today? Reading between the limes, he's smarting at being left of my honours list! My view is clear: never forget, never forgive. As Shakespeare's Henry III says, 'I am not in the giving vein today'.
Biceps oregano
Boris

Jun 25, 2023

Dear Mogg
There's public clarification that my pension for being PM is only £115k p.a. Now people can see I have been cast into penury like Little Dorritt in 'Little Women' and it is only by dent of my supreme oratorical skills I can scrape a living.
Ad lucre ad kleenex
Boris

Jun 29, 2023

Dear Mogg
Am horrified to see that a measly bunch of meddling bureaucrats have censured you and the gorgeous Nadine for undermining parliamentary procedure. And

MICHAEL ROSEN

you - such a stickler for such stuff! Lucky I got your knighthood sorted first!
Bonio cronio
Boris

Jun 29, 2023

Dear Mogg
I see that the High Court is dealing with how the govt and Baroness Hollett are at hoggerleads over my diaries. Think, if Samuel Peeps had had his diaries put through the legal mill, we might never have seen his insights into Victorian life.
Pepsi delirium
Boris

Jul 1, 2023

Dear Mogg
Sky News talks of me as the ghost still haunting Sunak! I so love that. Remember Macbeth sees the ghost of Banksie while all around see nothing? And it was Quentin Crisp who said, 'We are each our own devil, and we make this world our hell.'
Psoriasis in dahlia
Boris

Jul 1, 2023

Dear Mogg
My column in the Mail today is a plea for us to send the boats back to Rwanda. The Supreme Court will remember my article, bearing in mind my own adherence to all things legal. As one of Shakespeare's chaps says, 'Let's kill all the lawyers.'
Giotto con funghi
Boris

FARCE MAJEURE

Jul 1, 2023

Dear Eugeniusz
You have made the error of thinking that Michael Rosen wrote this letter. I wrote it and I know everything about Rwanda and other Latin countries of which it is a part.
Agricola cocacola
Boris

Jul 3, 2023

Dear Mogg
We're moving towards Royal Family status. The Bournemouth Echo reports on us thus: 'The family also had an ice cream during their visit.' Mundane acts made great by the grandeur of the actors. 'Even the ranks of Hungary could scarce forbear to cheer.'
Asda arcadia
Boris

Jul 4, 2023

Dear Mogg
The woke i rag is running a story how erstwhile colleagues in my beloved constituency of Oxbridge and Riuslip think they can win so long as they don't mention my name! Ah, but 'Thou canst not teach me to forget', as Romeo says to Hamlet.
Candelabra in sago
Boris

Jul 7, 2023

Dear Mogg
Every time I drop in on our side doing interviews or on QT and the like, I see that they've all started gabbling at 90 mph in some kind of strange disjointed burble. I

MICHAEL ROSEN

wasn't like that was I? They're not imitating me, are they?
Podium tedium
Boris

Jul 7, 2023

Dear Mogg
Am concerned how this WhatsUpp messages thingy is playing out. Baroness Hellett is going to be poring over some potentially unsavoury material. I thought the govt were going to win and she'd only get to see the redacted stuff!
Norma major
Boris

Shaun Wing replied:

Dear Boris
The old mare will learn something 'or three' - such as the best place to grab a green curry in the early hours without going through curry protocol Gastropo. After that the Baronet will likely "obdormiscere" - dream of Genie with Larry Grayson.
Sir Smugg

Jul 7, 2023

Dear Mogg
It is true that I once said that the Ultra Low Emission Zone was essential. It is also true that I now say I'm against the Ultra Low Emission Zone. I see no contradiction here.
Tina tuna
Boris

FARCE MAJEURE

Jul 7, 2023

Dear Mogg
Did you see my mock snore act? I am unique: one moment it's my tousled hair, the next my bum crack, the next our number 10 jollies. The point is, people don't want dullards. They want rumbustious heroes like me.
Max factor in toblerone
Boris

Jul 8, 2023

Dear Mogg
Note here that I am predicting that the General Election will be a debarcle for us and I have never made a wiser move than to abandon sheep. I have other chips to fry and as a result the world will benefit from my words of wisdom teeth.
Goretex in balti
Boris

Jul 9, 2023

Dear Mogg
We must back Biden on sending cluster bombs to Ukraine. They are like the triremes of Ancient Rome fired from their bows into the hearts of the savage Picts marauding northwards from Spain. Say no struggle might not availeth no nought.
Casus bellend
Boris

"The Robert Jenrick guide to Interior Design"

Financial Times - Jul 21, 2023

Most newspapers and news outlets had reported that Robert

MICHAEL ROSEN

Jenrick, the minister for immigration had ordered the painting over of Mickey Mouse murals at the asylum centre for lone children in Kent. Some gave a factual report, others tried a jokey response.

Jul 10, 2023

Dear Suella Braverman
I fear you have a Cultural Marxist close at hand. It's clear that Robert Jenrick painted over Mickey Mouse because he is a woke critic of the role of Disney in western culture. The enemy is within!
Respectfully yours
Michael Rosen

Jul 10, 2023

Dear Mogg
The woke mob are whinging that under my aegis it cost £800k for my prime ministerial plane to be painted with our great national flag. Worth every pinny, Moggo. As Mr Magoo the pilot said, 'I put out my hand and faced the God of touch.'
Aerosol anusol
Boris

Jul 15, 2023

Dear Mogg
Some hack has revealed that I earn £21k an hour. Hah! Some silly sods think they're doing well on £21 an hour! As Mercutio says in 'Twelfth Night', 'Some have greatness thrust upon them.' And I've thrust my greatness on others in my time too.
Interflora balti
Boris

FARCE MAJEURE

Three bi-elections were to take place on the 20th July owing to three Conservative Members of Parliament stepping down. Boris Johnson, the former Prime Minister, MP for Uxbridge and Ruislip; Nigel Adams, a supporter of Boris Johnson, MP for Selby and Ainsty; and David Warburton who had been suspended from the conservative party for taking cocaine and allegations of mis-conduct. He was MP for Somerton and Frome.

Jul 20, 2023

Dear Mogg
I predict a thumping win for us in my old beloved constituency of Oxbridge and Riuslip. My erstwhile constituents will remember me through rose-tainted glasses, as with the old Elton John song 'Memory' from the musical '42nd Street'.
Bon jovi in polo
Boris

"Tories keep hold of Boris Johnson's old seat in massive blow to Keir Starmer"

The Sun - Jul 21, 2023

They do not report the loss of Selby and Ainsty. The actual majority for the new Conservative member, Steve Tuckwell was 495.

Jul 21, 2023

Dear Mogg
As I predicted, my beloved Oxbridge and Riuslip stood by me, and turned in a thumping victory for us. What should this tell Sunak? Where there's Boris, we win. As Norma Jeane sang, 'I am a candle in the mind'. Julius

MICHAEL ROSEN

Iglesias Caesar
Boris

Jul 21, 2023

Dear Mogg
As the dust settles on this round of by-election results, the nation and Nadine turn to me to lift them out of the cloud of sand the nation finds itself in. The Party will summon me yet again - lovely old Boris, tousled hair and bum crack aloft.
Cloaca al fresco
Boris

Jul 22, 2023

Dear Mogg
The by-election failures are good for me. As the Westminster escalator takes off into the General Election dawn, the polls tell our great Party that there is only one way to get out the hole: with Boris.
Turbo turbot
Boris

Jul 22, 2023

Dear Mogg
If destiny's wheel shakes the dice of the hourglass in such a way that my legacy will not be as this nation's great leader but as a supreme orator striding the surface of the globe like the Jeremy Clarkson of conference jollies, so be it.
Ars longa ryvita brevis
Boris

FARCE MAJEURE

> Jul 22, 2023

Dear Mogg
I am lightly concerned with what they're going to find on my phone. Aside from the team selection I sent to the England Rugger HQ, I did express a candid view that this corona flu thing shouldn't interfere with the market.
Hummus interdens
Boris

Ro2o tweeted:

> To my friend Boris
> Were you really in a coma when you got corona virus? I can't believe such a healthy person as you could be get this virus. I believe you just needed a rest and went holiday. Why not we all deserve a break.
> Your friend Moggy

> Jul 22, 2023

Dear Mogg
My little chap, Ross Plimsole is now Baron Plimsole of Letchworth, a 31 year old sitting right there in Westminster, funnelling all my aperçuz through to the hacks. Look him up. Great little chappie. He is my aide de con.
Dexter in perspex
Boris

> Jul 24, 2023

Dear Mogg
The appalling Ferdinand Mount has written a book about Julius Caesar, Hitler and me. I suppose he thinks this is clever. One day when the chips are down and there's more fish in the sea, Mount and his cronies will be mere

MICHAEL ROSEN

wind in the straws.
Hydro electric kebab
Boris

Jul 25, 2023

Dear Mogg
Outrageous rumours circulating concerning my honours list and the peerage of a highly talented woman. People seem to think they can take a shop-pot at me with no concern for truth. As Thelonius says to Hamlet 'To thine own self be true'.
In flagrante predicto
Boris

Jul 27, 2023

Dear Mogg
I shun tattle-tittle about my personal life but I was delighted to let Hello Mag in to see our gorgeous house and garden and homemade crumble. The caricature of me as a dissolute monied fop disappears under this rosy glimpse of domesticity.
Acacia in rectum
Boris

Jul 28, 2023

Dear Nadine
Far be it from me to make any kind of criticism of your conduct, but it has come to my notice that there is a soupçong of a contradiction in your present position. In short, you said you were gonna quit but you ain't quit, as Malvolio put it.
Quid pro quack
Boris

FARCE MAJEURE

                                                          Jul 28, 2023

Dear Mogg
I was on the sauce last night and can't remember what the fuss is about this Ulez thingy. Is it Oil of Ulez that some of the female members of my entourage wear? Answer by return, Moggo.
Info con mayo
Boris

                                                          Jul 30, 2023

Dear Mogg
In my column in the Mail I provide a glossary to my use of Latinate words: eg Homunculus (plural homunculi). This way, I not only show that I am brilliant but also that I make the effort to educate the feeble-minded readers.
Feliciti kendali
Boris

                                                          Aug 1, 2023

Dear Mogg
The more I seek Arcadia, the more I am beset with pettyfogging twerps: my plan for a pool menaced by steely-faced bureaucrats defending newt rights! Remember the irony of 'O brave new world that hath such people in it,' (Amanda in 'The Tempest').
Revlon in crisis
Boris

MICHAEL ROSEN

Aug 9, 2023

Dear Mogg
I see our great party slipping out of power like a plug in a tool box. We should be seizing the ball by the horns just as England's greatest rugger player Brian O'Driscoll did. Only Suella Bravuraman senses the danger we're in.
Hypochondria in hydrangea
Boris

Aug 14, 2023

Dear Mogg
The rumour in the bullrushes is that the odious Venusioid Dominic Cummings, is on the verge of starting up a new political party. He will die in the splatter of verbal napalm from me and my juggernaut of fans.
Venus in hummus
Boris

FARCE MAJEURE

MICHAEL ROSEN

Photo by Billie Charity - Hay Festival 2022

Michael Rosen is one of Britain's best loved writers and performance poets for children and adults. He was Children's Laureate from 2007-2009. In 2023 he has been awarded the PEN Pinter Prize. It is awarded annually to a writer whose body of work shows a "fierce intellectual determination...to define the real truth of our lives and our societies".

His first degree in English Literature and Language was from Wadham College, Oxford and he went on to study for an MA at the University of Reading and a PhD at the former University of North London, now London Metropolitan. He is currently Professor of Children's Literature at Goldsmith, University of London where he co-devised and teaches critical approaches to reading on an MA course in Children's Literature, having done the same at Birbeck, University of London.

In 2021 he received the annual J.M. Barrie Lifetime Achievement Award from the charity, Action for Children's Arts. In 2022 he was awarded an honorary fellowship of the Royal College of Nursing for support for nursing and advocacy for patients including those suffering with Long Covid-19.

He frequently gives talks and presents radio programmes on the BBC. Currently he is the presenter of the popular programme 'Word of Mouth' on Radio 4. He champions poetry and other poets on YouTube channels.